The Scullery Maid's Success

A riveting Victorian family saga

Emily Catford

Contents

Chapter 1

"Please dad, stop!" Jane pleaded.

Fred stopped for a second, visibly angry, then hit Mary again and again, until his energy was spent. Then he stood there huffing and puffing for a while until he stumbled out of the kitchen towards the bedroom where no doubt, he would fall into a stupor as he did most evenings.

Jane ran to her mother who had curled up against the wall in a small ball to try and protect herself from the worst of the beating. Mary was a slight woman, with pale blue eyes and long straight hair that was usually pulled back into a tight bun. She had once been quite beautiful, but the years of living with Fred had taken their toll.

"Are you okay?" she asked, with a worried look in the same pale blue eyes her mother had.

"I'm fine love, don't worry about me. I'm used to it by now. Why don't you put the kettle on and make us both a nice cup of tea?"

Jane moved over to the kettle and lit the fire underneath it. She was glad that her mum was okay, but was worried that one day her father would go too far and her mum might not come out of it unscathed.

While she was making the tea, Mary looked over to her. Her daughter was growing into a fine young woman and she was proud of how she was turning out. She was so kind to everyone and was always lending a helping hand to their neighbours. Thankfully Fred's cruelty hadn't affected her temperament.

Jane looked up. "Are you sure you're okay?"

"Yes, don't worry. I'm just glad it was me, not you this time."

Fred was a large man, with broad shoulders and a thick neck. He had a nasty temper at the best of times, but since he had lost his job at the cotton mill it had got ten times worse. Especially, as he spent all their spare change on ale. He mostly took it out on Mary, but occasionally Jane would say the wrong thing or be in the wrong place and she would feel the full force of her father's hand.

Jane and Mary sat at the table, quietly sipping their tea, thinking about next week, when Jane would be leaving the family home to take up the position of scullery maid in a big house in the neighbouring town.

"What's going to happen when I'm gone? How will you cope?" Jane fretted.

"Jane, stop worrying. I'll be fine. If it gets too bad, I'll run to a neighbour's house and hide out there until your father has calmed down. Everything will work itself out. Just you think about your new job and how you can make a good impression on the family while you're there."

Jane nodded, but couldn't stop worrying. While she was around, she could help defend her mum from Fred, but if she wasn't there, who knew what would happen. However, she knew her mum needed the money that Jane would be earning. Since Fred had lost his job, the only wages coming in were those that Mary got from taking in washing and ironing from some of the bigger houses on the edge of town and Fred spent most of that money on booze.

Jane was going to send Mary every penny that she earned and hoped that one day she'd be able to persuade her mum to leave Fred for a happier and more peaceful life. In the meantime, she was determined to find a way to look after her mum even if she wasn't around to do so.

The next day she went around to the neighbour's house to have a quiet word with him. She wanted to ask him to keep an eye out for Mary now that Jane wouldn't be there to protect her. She knocked on the door and waited patiently. Harry opened the door slowly and peaked out.

"Oh, hello Jane. Come in, come in. What can I do for you this fine morning?"

"Hello Mr Bennett, I've come to ask you a favour actually." She replied hesitantly.

Jane knew Harry was a gentle man. He was quite tall and slender, with wire-framed glasses that he often looked over the top of, rather than remove them. He was kind and thoughtful to his neighbours and always had a smile for Jane. He was a school teacher and many a time had arisen, when she had knocked on his door when she was little, scared because her father was beating on her mother. Harry had always welcomed her in and told her short stories to try to comfort her. As she had gotten older, he had taught her to read and write, which she took to quite easily.

Harry showed her into the kitchen.

"So, what can I do for you?" he asked.

"Well, it's my mum."

"Yes?"

"Well, I'm going to be leaving early next week to take up my position as a scullery maid, and I'm worried about what's going to happen to mum." She explained.

"Go on," Harry said, wondering exactly what Jane was going to ask of him.

"I was wondering, would you just keep an ear out for her and if you think it's getting too bad next door, would you mind going next door and perhaps knocking on the pretence of needing some sugar or something..." Jane's voice trailed off softly.

She wasn't sure what she expected of Harry. She hadn't thought it all through exactly. She just knew that she couldn't leave without doing something.

Harry, like most of their neighbours, knew what Fred was like and how he treated Mary. He had always tried to help Mary when he could and though he was surprised that Jane had sought him out to ask the question, he didn't blame her for making the request.

Harry smiled at her. "Well, I can't promise anything. But I will keep an ear out and do my best to be there if your mother needs me. She's a kindly soul and doesn't deserve to be treated so badly."

Jane left Harry's house knowing that she'd done everything she could before leaving, but couldn't help feeling apprehensive about what would happen in her absence.

The week passed quickly and before she knew it, she was off to start up her new position. Her father was out when she left, and her mum cried buckets of tears.

"I'm going to miss you so much." She sobbed.

"I won't go if you don't want me to."

"Don't take any notice of this silly old woman. Of course, you must go. You're meant for much better things that you'll get here. You must take advantage of the opportunity. I'll be okay."

Jane put her few belongings in a bag and gave her mum a big hug as they both cried softly. She knew she would miss her mum, but she was excited and nervous as she left the house for the next chapter in her life.

Chapter 2

Billy was sat at the table eating his breakfast before leaving for the cotton mill. He looked over to his adoptive mother and smiled gently at her. Clara had always been quite plump and as she got older became quite matronly and was hardly ever seen without her apron on and a cloth in her hand. She was a kindly soul and doted on both Billy and her husband Sam.

"What?" She asked.

"Nothing." He replied.

Clara smiled to herself. The day that the vicar had told them about the baby that had been left on the church steps had been a good day. She and Sam had been overjoyed. They had been unable to have a child of their own and were getting older. This had been their last chance to have a baby and they loved him as though he was their own flesh and blood.

"What are you thinking about?" asked Billy, fully knowing that she was reminiscing again. He knew she was fond of the memories of him as a baby and had loved telling him the story of how they had come to be his parents, often romanticising about the way the vicar had given them the gift of parenthood.

"You know full well what I'm thinking about." She laughed. "I was just remembering you as a baby. That full head of white-blond hair and those beautiful blue eyes that looked up at me so trustingly. We were so happy to have you and to bring you home with us. I can't believe that you're so dark now that you are older." She said as she ruffled his now nearly black hair.

Billy grinned at her as he stood up, ready to get off to work. "Dad already left?" he asked.

"Yeah, he wanted to call in to see how Joe was on the way to work. Make sure he's okay after his accident last week."

Billy nodded sadly. Joe was a mule scavenger and had nearly fallen into the machine as he was collecting the cotton. Luckily, someone had caught his arm and dragged him back before he did himself terrible damage. That was one of the many problems at the mill. They wouldn't waste the cotton that fell under the machine, so they employed children to go underneath them, while they were still running to collect the cotton and clean the floors. There had been quite a few near-death accidents, in the short time that Billy had been working there.

Billy grabbed the sandwich that his mother had prepped and wrapped ready for him to take and pushed it into his pocket. He gave Clara a quick peck on the top of her head and wished her a good day, before leaving the house.

It was still dark, and the morning mist hung in the air. Billy pulled up the collar of his jacket and shivered as the cold air started to penetrate through his thin outer layers. He picked up his pace in order to warm himself and as he neared the mill, he caught up with Sam who was just leaving Joe's house.

"Morning dad. How is he?" Billy asked.

"Morning son. Not so bad, I don't suppose. He's still shaken up, as you might well understand. He is scared of going back, but his ma and pa need him to, so I think they're expecting him to be back at the mill tomorrow."

Billy nodded at his father. He knew that most families around here didn't have much. They needed to send out their children to work in the factories and mills so there was enough money to feed them all. Without it, they would be in danger of going to the workhouse. But still, he did feel sorry for poor Joe. Luckily Sam and Clara had managed without Billy going into the mill until he was older, so he never had to do the work of a mule scavenger. For that, he was ever grateful.

They entered the mill and went their separate ways, ready for the day ahead. Billy didn't like his job much, but he was happy to be working and earning a full week's wage. It allowed him to contribute to his family's income and to thank them for all they had done. He would do any work, no matter how humble, even though he knew he could never fully repay their love and care over the years.

Chapter 3

When Jane arrived to take up her new position at Osborne House, she was greeted by a young girl who showed her into the kitchen.

"Hello, my dear" said a rather rotund woman with a cheerful smile on her face. "You Jane?"

"Yes." Stammered Jane.

"Well, I'm Cook and I'll be the one telling you what to do." She explained.

Jane nodded.

"Come along child, I don't bite." She laughed.

Jane looked around for somewhere to put her bag. Cook seeing her confused said, "Just put it down on that chair and I'll get Daisy to show you your bed in a bit and you can take it then."

Jane nervously put down her bag and followed Cook further into the kitchen. Cook showed her around and told her main duties and left her to get on with it. She turned to the ovens where she was preparing breakfast for the family upstairs, who were going to be making an appearance in the dining room in a short while.

As Jane worked, she looked around her at her new surroundings. It was all so foreign to her. At home, they had a small fire where they did most of the cooking, but here the ovens were so big and the food looked so different than the bread and dripping Jane normally had for breakfast. She knew she was going to miss her mum dreadfully, but she felt quite excited to be starting on this new adventure.

Jane scrubbed the kitchen floors, washed the cutlery, crockery, and glassware until it shone and by the end of the day, she was grubby and exhausted. Cook had been keeping an eye on her all day and was pleased with her hard-working attitude. *Yes, she'll do okay.* She thought.

Cook turned to Jane and asked, "So, what did you think of your first day then lass?"

"Oh, it's hard work, but I really enjoyed it. Everyone seems to be kind and happy to show me the ropes. I think I'll get on grand, Cook"

"I think you're right." Replied Cook. "Now, you have an early start in the morning. You'll need to get up and help Daisy here to light the fires, so go along and get yourself some sleep."

Daisy turned out to be the young girl that had shown Jane in, and they were sharing a small bedroom, no bigger than a broom cupboard. She led Jane down a small corridor, where Jane put down her bag and changed into her nightdress, before slipping under the covers and falling into an exhausted sleep.

As the weeks went on, Jane settled into her new life. She missed her mum and worried about how she was getting on with her dad, without Jane there to smooth things over. However, she enjoyed being in the company of the small group of servants and seeing how the other half lived. She especially liked Daisy, who turned out to be older than she looked, with a gentle disposition and a friendly ear.

Her days would start early and finish late but at the end of each month, she would take a full day to go and see her mum and hand over her wages. She tried to time it with her dad leaving the house to go and visit his mate down the road. This way her mum could secretly pocket some of the money before her dad had realised Jane had been there.

She wasn't always so lucky in her timing and if her dad was home, he would grab the money from Jane and her mum wouldn't see sight of it.

These were the times when he would get even drunker than normal and Jane would be on tenterhooks not knowing whether his mood would change. During these visits, Jane would plead with her mum to leave him and find somewhere else to go, but her mum never would.

One Sunday as she was returning to Osborne House. She turned the corner towards the servant's entrance and bumped into a young man. She looked up at a rather handsome man and apologised "Sorry sir, I didn't see you coming."

The young man looked at her and leered. "That's okay, I'm always happy to bump into a pretty little lady like yourself."

Jane looked around worriedly. She was all alone and didn't know what to do. She was unfamiliar with this situation. Although she was aware that some boys in her village would look at her while she walked down the street, no one had ever been so direct in their approach.

The young man laughed. "Where are you going?" he asked.

"I'm the scullery maid here at this house." She said turning towards the house and pointing.

"Oh, that's good. It means we might see more of each other. You see I'm John. I live here with my father, so there's every chance we could bump into each other quite often."

He towered over her, a little too close for her liking, and so she said nervously "Yes sir, well I'd better be going. Cook will be expecting me back, and I don't want to get into trouble. Goodbye, sir."

John moved to one side and Jane scurried off to the kitchen.

"What is it child?" asked Cook, on seeing her looking so anxious.

"I've just bumped into someone. They said their name was John, and they live here..." Jane replied, hoping it wasn't true.

Cook interrupted her. "Yes, John is the son of Mr Morgan and you don't have to say another word. I know exactly how you're feeling. You won't be the first servant that John has taken a liking to. Well, don't worry, I'll keep an eye out for you."

Jane felt comforted by these words, but deep inside her stomach was an uncomfortable feeling that she couldn't quite shake.

Chapter 4

Jane tried to keep out of John's way and for the most part this was easy. She was confined to the kitchen and servant's quarters, where she rarely saw any of the family. In time she settled down and forgot about John. Her work was so tiring that she didn't have much time to do anything except work and sleep.

Until the day that Cook asked Jane to go and fetch Daisy, who had recently taken over the role of chambermaid and as such was upstairs, taking hot water into the family's rooms. Jane started up the stairs and was walking along a corridor when she realised that she must have taken a wrong turn somewhere. Daisy was nowhere to be found and Jane quickly turned to retrace her steps, when she ran smack into John.

"Why hello," John said.

"Hello, sir." She replied anxiously.

"What brings you to my quarters?"

"Oh, sir I'm so sorry. I was looking for Daisy and I've got myself all lost."

John sidled over a little closer until he was almost stood over her.

"That's good news for me, my pretty."

Jane backed away nervously until her back hit the wall behind her.

"Well, I better go sir."

"What's the hurry? We could make each other very happy."

Jane didn't really know what he meant but didn't like the tone in which he said it.

"Please, sir, I have to go. Cook will be wondering where I am."

With that Cook appeared and looking at John she said "Come on dear. What are you doing up here? Daisy is on the other side of the house. Come along. We have lots to do."

Grabbing Jane from beneath John's grasp, she hurried them both down to the kitchen.

"I'm sorry, Cook. I got lost and when I was coming back down, I bumped into him. I hadn't even known he was there." She stammered.

"That's okay child. You just need to be more careful. Goodness knows what would have happened if I hadn't turned up when I did. You need to keep out of his way."

Jane went back to her scrubbing, thankful to Cook for being so kind to her. As she was cleaning away the dinner things, she heard Cook and the footman talking about her.

"Poor girl. Catching the eye of that philanderer." Said Cook.

"Yes, and only a few months since Hannah had to be sent away after she got in the family way, thanks to that cad." Replied the footman.

"Well, let's hope that he goes back to London soon, and she doesn't have to be bothered by him. In the meantime, I'll try to ensure that Jane keeps downstairs, well out of his way."

Jane shot them a confused glance. What were they talking about? What had the young man been up to?

They looked over and seeing her watching them, gave her a kindly smile and went their separate ways.

Later in their room, Jane mentioned the whispered conversation to Daisy.

"What did they mean by it all?" she asked.

"Well," confided Daisy. "Hannah was the scullery maid before you. She was about our age and Master John took a liking to her. He wouldn't leave her alone. In the end, she was frightened to just leave the kitchen. It got so bad. Anyway, one day he collared her in the garden as she was leaving to visit her parents, and I don't know what happened, but a couple of months later, Hannah had to leave. She was expecting a baby. I think Mr Morgan gave her some money to set herself up.

"The master was sent to London to work in his father's company. It's only recently that he's been allowed back here, and apparently, so I've heard, under strict instructions to leave the servants alone. So, his father won't be best pleased if it comes to his attention that he's been trying to get friendly with you. He's a nasty piece of work you mark my words. Keep well away from him."

Jane was shocked. Daisy was usually a girl of few words. In fact, she didn't think she had ever heard her make such a long statement.

"Of course, I will Daisy. Don't worry about me. I can look after myself if I need to. But thanks for the warning. I will keep my wits about me when I leave the kitchens."

She sounded confident to Daisy, but in reality, she was scared of what might happen. She couldn't lose this job, her mum relied on the extra money coming in, plus her not living there, it was one less mouth to feed.

She tossed and turned all night, different scenarios going around her head, worrying about what she might do until she fell into a restless sleep. Before she knew it, morning had arrived, and she dragged herself out of bed ready to start the fires in the kitchen and just wanting to get the day over.

A couple of days later Jane heard that Master John had left for London, and she gave a huge sigh of relief. She wasn't sure whether someone had said something to Mr Morgan or if it had been a coincidence. Either way, she was grateful that she could relax, at least for the time being.

It was the end of the month so when Sunday came around Jane left to visit her mum. The first thing she noticed was the bruising around Mary's eyes and at the top of her arms.

"Oh mum, what happened?"

"The usual. I was late in putting the tea on the table and your dad was in a bit of a bad way, and you know…" her voice trailed off.

"You really should leave him," Jane said.

Her mum would always respond by telling Jane that Fred wasn't so bad really, that it was because he was frustrated by not being employed that he was in a temper so often. Jane knew this wasn't true as her dad had been like that ever since she could remember and had lost his job because of the drink. But she would never rebuke her mum, preferring to turn the conversation to happier topics.

Luckily Fred kept away from the house while Jane was there and far too soon for the both of them, it was time for Jane to make her way back to Osbourne House.

She pondered on things as she walked quickly back the way she'd come just a few hours earlier. Life seemed to have taken on a methodical and steady state and Jane wondered if there was more to look forward to than the daily grind that seemed to have become her life.

As she was deep in thought, she heard a man's voice saying "Hello."

She looked up and saw a kind dark-haired man of about her age. She replied, "Hello, can I help you?"

"I was wondering if you could direct me to Claypool Lane?"

"Of course." Replied Jane. "It's just along there, the second on the left."

"Thank you." Said Billy. "I'm just doing a few chores for my mum and this is the last place I need to go."

Jane smiled at him and told him it was the same direction she was going in, so she would walk along with him if that was okay. Somehow, she didn't want to leave his company just yet. Even though she had only just met him, she felt in him a kindred spirit.

As for Billy, he knew where the road was but had seen Jane and wanted to speak with her and used this question as an excuse to start a conversation.

They walked towards the lane indulging in light conversation and thoroughly enjoying each other's company. All too soon, they reached the turning and Billy turned to Jane and said "This is me then, I believe."

Jane smiled, agreed that it was, and went to take her leave.

"Wait." Said Billy. "Would it be okay to see you again?"

"Yes." Replied Jane blushing.

They arranged to meet the following Sunday when Jane had a half day. Jane continued onto the House, while Billy tripped up Claypool Lane happy that he'd met such a nice girl.

She walked into the kitchen dreamily and Cook noticed her and asked "So child, what's going on? I bet it involves a young man." She smiled knowingly.

"Yes." Replied Jane. "I've just met a delightful young man. He was very handsome and kind. We've arranged to meet again next week."

"Well, be careful." Warned Cook. "You've only just met him."

Jane smiled knowing instinctively that Billy would never hurt her and was looking forward to when Sunday would come again.

Chapter 5

The following Sunday saw Jane meeting Billy at the nearby park. The sun was shining and the air felt warm on their faces. It was a perfect day and Jane was pleasantly surprised how easy she felt in Billy's company. They took a lovely stroll, meandering through the park, stopping to look at the ducks in the pond and the squirrels chasing each other up and down the trees. They took a few breaks, sitting on the park benches to take a breath and even stopped for ice cream.

They chatted about all types of things and nothing felt off-limits. Billy wasn't sure how it happened but he found himself telling Jane how he had been adopted at birth. As he was recounting the tale, he felt nervous that she might find it off-putting and think of an excuse to leave as soon as possible. But he shouldn't have worried.

"How exciting. Have you ever thought about looking for your real parents?"

"As far as I'm concerned, they are my real parents. They've certainly looked after me as such. But yes, I do sometimes wonder who left me at the church and why. I'm not sure that I'll ever find out though."

Jane agreed. It would be extremely unlikely that anyone would come forwards now and with the vicar long deceased, there was no link to the past for Billy to unpick.

Conversation turned to lighter topics and all too quickly it was time for Jane to get back to the House.

Billy walked her back and they agreed to meet again the following week.

"I've had a lovely day." Said Billy.

"Me too." Smiled Jane.

"I can't wait for next time, maybe we could go for tea somewhere, or maybe even a show?"

"That would be nice." Said Jane.

"Until next Sunday then." Replied Billy. He was happy just to be in her company. He wanted to kiss her but thought it might be too soon, so he said goodbye and turned to leave her.

Jane watched him strolling away and wished that he had kissed her. It would have been her first time, but she knew that it would have been magical. As he turned the corner he looked back and saw her watching him. He felt butterflies in his stomach. *Is this what love feels like?* He thought as he gave her a hearty wave and saw her happily return it. He continued back home, deep in contemplation and excitement about their next encounter.

Jane reluctantly turned and returned to the kitchen, where Daisy gave her a quick wink and said "So...?"

Jane whirled around excitedly. "It was okay I suppose." She grinned.

"I want more gossip than that." Laughed Daisy.

Jane told her all about the afternoon, but left out the part about Billy's heritage. She didn't think that it was her story to tell. Cook listened happily to the young girls chatting as she busily prepared the vegetables for the evening meal. After a while though, she turned to them and said indulgently "That's enough now girls. Get on with your work, otherwise, I'll have to come at you with the broom."

The girls laughed knowing that Cook was joking, but at the same time, they stopped chatting and got on with their work. They knew that if they didn't, it would just delay the time they could go to bed and that was a luxury they didn't want to miss out on.

Later, once they were settled in their beds, Daisy asked "So, you like Billy then?"

"Yes, I do believe I do."

"Is it serious?"

"It's too soon to say, I think. I really like him, but I've only just met him and who knows how it will turn out. Besides, aren't I a little young to think about settling down just yet?"

As she finished talking, she heard a soft snore coming from the bed next to her. Exhaustion had overtaken Daisy, and she was fast asleep and hadn't heard Jane's final words. Jane laughed softly to herself and found herself pondering the question of what she wanted from life, before dropping off into a deep sleep.

Chapter 6

The week went quickly. They got up at dawn every day to light the fires, get the hot water prepared for upstairs, cleaned and generally did whatever they were told to do. They'd go to sleep each evening feeling exhausted and Sunday soon came around again.

Jane quickly did her chores excited that she was meeting Billy again later. They spent another lovely afternoon strolling in the park. Billy picked Jane a bunch of wild flowers which she carried around all day.

"I love the way the sun shines through the petals, giving them such a pretty glow." She said

Billy smiled, thinking that she looked just like one of those flowers. "Yes, it does. doesn't it."

Jane noticed his admiring glance and blushed. She loved the way that her stomach did somersaults when she looked at him, but she wasn't used to such attention and said shyly "Do you think we could walk to the bandstand to see if anyone is playing?"

"What a great idea. Do you like music?" Billy asked

"I haven't really heard much, but yes, I think I might." She replied

They walked along to the bandstand and there was a small brass band playing.

"Oh, how exciting." Jane said

Billy smiled. He liked the band, but he was more interested in watching her.

They spent another hour listening to the music and chatting together, before it was time for Jane to get back. Billy walked with her, holding her arm and keeping close, not wanting to let her go just yet.

"I've got to help my dad next Sunday," said Billy, what about the following week?"

"Oh, I can't. That is the day I go to my mums." Jane replied disappointed.

"Well, we will just have to bide our time and wait until the week after, I suppose." Said Billy.

"You do still want to meet, don't you?"

"Oh, yes, more than anything," Jane replied, then quickly put her hand over her mouth, embarrassed that she'd shown quite how much she looked forward to their rendezvous.

Billy's heart jumped into his mouth. She feels the same way as I do. He thought.

"Good. Well, that's settled then. We'll meet at the gates in three Sundays."

They made their goodbyes and Billy reluctantly left Jane to go indoors. He turned, thinking about their day together, knowing he was falling in love with her.

Pay day came again and so Jane was going back to her mums. I know I shouldn't think it, but I do hope dad isn't in. she thought, It's nice to see mum, but dad always seems to be able to spoil any enjoyment we get from the visit.

She set off quite early in order to spend as much time with her mum as possible. It was a lovely day and as she walked through town, she could smell the scent of freshly baked bread coming from the bakery. She felt quite hungry and was tempted to spend a little of her wages on a quarter loaf of bread, so she could tear a little off before she got home.

But in the end, she wanted to make sure her mum had all her wages, so she ignored the rumblings and marched on to the next village.

She got home quite quickly so would be able to have a good few hours with her mum before she would have to make the return trip to get back to Osbourne House.

"Hello" she called out as she pushed open the door.

Her mum looked up from her sewing and smiled. "Hello child. Aren't you a sight for sore eyes? Let me take a proper look at you." She said standing up to go to Jane to give her a hug.

"There's something different about you?" she said after giving her the once over.

"Come on spit it out girl, is it a boy?"

Jane laughed. Her mum knew her so well. "Sit down mum. I'll put the kettle on and tell you all about it."

She went over to the kettle that was hanging over the fire keeping the water hot. She poured them both a cup of weak tea and took them over to where her mum was sitting and sat down on the floor beside her.

"Come on then child, tell me all about it. It's got to be a boy. You have a real sparkle in your eyes."

Jane blushed. "His name's Billy. He works at the cotton mill not far from where I'm working." We went out for a walk last Sunday and oh, mum I felt like I could talk to him about anything."

Her mum smiled indulgently. "Sounds wonderful. So, is he good looking, what are his parents like? Tell me everything you know."

As Jane was filling her mum in on all the details the front door pushed open and there was her dad. He caught the tail end of the conversation and exploded.

"You are far too young to be getting involved with men. You should be concentrating on your work, on making a good impression, and maybe even moving up to a kitchen maid before you start thinking about marriage. I'm not having you come back here telling me you are in the family way. You need to stay away from him until you are old enough."

What he meant though, was that if Jane got married, then they'd stop getting her wages. He knew they relied on that money.

"I forbid you to see him again. You hear me?" he roared.

He towered over Jane and she crouched down, fearful that he was going to hit her. But the punch never came. He knew that if she returned to the House bruised and battered that someone would say something and he didn't want anyone messing around in his business.

"I said, did you hear me?" a spittle-laden shout pierced her ears.

"Yes, dad. I understand. I'm sorry. I won't see him again." She said sobbing into her mum's skirts.

Chapter 7

H e stormed back out the way he'd come.

"There, there." Mary said, patting Jane's head.

"Ignore him. If you like this boy, then by all means take walks in the park with him. There's no harm in it and anyway, how's your dad going to find out about it. The only two places he spends any time at are here and The Bull."

Jane's sobs softened, becoming sniffles and then hiccups as she got herself together again. "I know you're right mum, it's just that I was hoping to bring him here to meet you sometime and now I won't be able to. It's not fair."

"Hush child. It'll be okay. He'll come around eventually. You know he'll have to."

Jane wasn't convinced but there was nothing more to do about it and so she changed the subject. "Why do you stay with him, mum? He's cruel and nasty to you and takes all your money and gives nothing in return."

"I've made my bed and I'll lie in it." Her mum replied as she did every time that Jane mentioned it. "Anyway, where would I go? Your grandparents have passed and I don't have any other family that I know of. I'm stuck here and most of the time he's not too bad. It's just when the gets the beer inside him."

"And that more often than not now mum. Really, you should..."

Jane's mum interrupted her. "Now Jane, let's talk about something nicer. Tell me all about your job and Cook. Tell me, is Daisy as nice as you thought she was?"

Jane sighed; her mum wasn't about to change her mind. She was wasting her breath. So, she nodded and started talking excitedly about how nice Cook was, how she let her help prepare the vegetables sometimes, and even let her stir the soup on occasion. Daisy was terrific, Jane couldn't think of a better roommate.

Her mum smiled and let Jane's enthusiastic deluge of information wash over her. She was delighted that her daughter had got the job and was spending time with people her own age. Most of all she was relieved that she had managed to get away from the toxic situation that Fred had created here in this small crumbly room.

All too soon it was time to take the long walk back to Osbourne House if she wasn't to be late. She hugged her mum tightly and passed over her wages. "Bye mum. I'll miss you."

"Me too child. It's gone far too quickly, but don't forget what I said. Carry on walking out with Billy and everything will sort itself out at some point."

Mary stood at the door, waving until Jane was out of sight.

On the way back Jane's thoughts drifted to Billy. Some of what her dad had said made sense. She was still quite young and maybe she could better herself in some way. *What if Billy wasn't the right person for her.*

How can I know whether what I'm feeling is love, or just infatuation? She thought. *I don't know him that well and what if he turns out to be like dad? After all, mum told me that dad wasn't always like that, that he'd changed once they'd been married a few months. What if Billy's the same? I don't think I could cope.*

She felt quite confused with it all. On the way over, she hadn't been able to wait to tell her mum all about Billy and how much she liked him. Now she was stomping back dejectedly, not knowing what to do about it all. It was all too much.

She put her head around the kitchen door to let Cook know that she had returned.

"Gosh, look at that face!" exclaimed Cook. "You look like you lost a shilling and found sixpence. What's happened? Is your mum okay?"

No one knew much about Jane's family, but Cook had picked up on the different ways that Jane spoke about her family and had noticed that she always clammed up when someone asked her about her dad. So, although she didn't know the details, she did know there was no love lost there.

"Yes, Cook." Replied Jane, "Everything's fine. I'm just tired, that's all. I think I'll go on up to bed, if you don't mind?"

"Of course not. You've got an early start in the morning, and it wouldn't do for you to be getting up late, now would it." Cook responded gently.

"Goodnight Cook."

"Goodnight."

Jane pulled herself up the stairs. She hadn't exactly lied to Cook, but she hadn't told her the whole truth. She did feel bad about it, but this was her problem and something she'd have to deal with herself.

She collapsed on the bed feeling exhausted. Luckily Daisy hadn't returned yet, so there were no awkward questions from that end. She led there, head spinning with all the questions she had, with no way of knowing if she would make the right decision. *I'll leave it until next Sunday,* she thought, *and maybe when I see Billy it will all be much clearer.*

Billy was on the other side of town, lying on his bed thinking about Jane oblivious that she was having second thoughts. *Should I tell her how I feel about her next time we meet or is it too soon? I don't want to scare her off. Maybe I should wait a while, but I just want to shout it from the hilltops. I want her to know that I love her and want to marry her as soon as possible.*

Chapter 8

She heard Daisy come in a little later, but didn't feel like talking, so pretended to be asleep when she whispered over to her. It took a long time to drift off, but eventually, she fell into a deep but troubled sleep.

The next day she dragged herself out of bed. "You look awful." Said Daisy

"I'm fine, I just didn't sleep well."

"That's odd, you were asleep when I got in."

"Yes, well I woke in the middle of the night and couldn't get back to sleep," Jane said, telling a small lie, not wanting to admit that she had been pretending to be asleep the night before.

So that Daisy didn't start asking about her day off, Jane got dressed and briskly disappeared downstairs. Daisy thought it was a bit odd, but soon threw herself into her job and promptly forgot about it.

It wasn't until later that evening when they were preparing themselves for bed that Daisy managed to ask Jane how she was. Jane explained how her dad had forbidden her to see Billy again, but that her mum had been on her side.

"Oh, you poor thing. What are you going to do?"

"I don't know. I think I will talk with Billy and see what he says. Maybe that will give me an idea of his true character. Then I can make up my mind."

Daisy agreed that this was a very good idea and Jane slept much easier after sharing her worries with her friend.

The week seemed to drag by, but finally, it was Sunday. Billy had arranged to meet Jane at the gates leading into the garden. He was prompt, not wishing to waste any of the precious time he would spend with Jane.

Jane woke up early and got ready nervously. "You'll be fine," Daisy told her encouragingly. "just talk with Billy and see how the land lies. Then you'll know what to do and you know I'll be here when you get back if you need me." She pushed Jane towards the door and smiled saying "Good luck."

Jane slowly descended the stairs and went out the back door, still not knowing what was going to happen. She saw Billy waiting for her and her heart leaped. In that instance, she knew she loved him and her only hope was that he felt the same way about her. His face lit up as he saw her hurrying towards him. He decided right there and then, he was going to tell her how he felt.

As they were saying getting reacquainted at the garden gates Jane noticed the lady of the house looking down at them. "Who is that?" asked Billy

"That's Mrs Morgan." Replied Jane

"Why's she looking at us so intently?"

"I've no idea, but yes, she is isn't she."

"No matter. Let's go to the park if that's okay with you?" he asked gently. "And maybe I'll treat you to another ice cream if you're lucky."

Billy took her arm and gently led Jane to the park, where they spent the afternoon together, listening to the band and meandering gently through the park, appreciating the nature that was all around them.

As Alice noticed them looking back up to her and she pulled quickly away from the window trembling. *How can it be?* she thought to herself shakily. *Has he found me and is going to blackmail me to stop him telling my secret?*

She found the nearest chair and sunk into it fretting to herself. There was no doubt though. *He is the spitting image of her younger brother. There was no way that he isn't her son. But how did he get to be standing at the gates of their house and what does he want?*

Alice thought back to when she was just nineteen years old. She had been so much in love. They had been engaged to be married, and she thought that nothing could go wrong. Until it did. And when it did, it went horribly wrong. Her fiancé had died suddenly after contracting cholera. She had found herself pregnant with his son and hadn't known what to do.

Her best friend had been absolutely brilliant. She had arranged for them to stay at her relative's home, and they had told Alice's family that they were going to spend a few months at her aunts to look after her while she was convalescing. In actual fact, she was holidaying abroad for the winter and knew nothing about the stay.

They had spent a couple of months there, hiding out so that no one would know that they were there. They had come with some provisions and had hired a local boy to get fresh produce for them while they were there. The time had passed really slowly, with every day bringing the worry of being found out by someone.

The baby had been born at home, with a local midwife being called in and sworn to secrecy. Jane had been so upset. It wasn't an easy birth, and she was so worried that she would have to go to the hospital. Eventually, though it was over and this big bouncy boy arrived. He had a beautiful head of hair and the heartiest set of lungs. Jane wasn't sure whether she was going to be able to go ahead with their plans. But once the baby was a few weeks old they had wrapped him up well and crept down to the church leaving him on the church steps an hour before they knew the vicar would be opening the church for Sunday service.

Alice had felt horrible about it but hadn't seen any other way. Her parents would have disowned her if they had known about it and she certainly wouldn't be sitting here now, happily married to dear Ron. The guilt had eaten at her continuously until one year later she had revisited the church and confessed what she had done to the vicar.

Unfortunately, the vicar had no news for her. A couple had adopted the baby quite quickly after the vicar had found him. They were a kindly couple who couldn't have a child of their own. They had left for an unknown destination quite soon after. Maybe because they were worried that the boy's real parents would come to claim him as their own.

It was too late. Alice was heartbroken and returned home as a different woman. It took a long time to get over it, but eventually, she met Ron, who was a widow older than herself, but so kind and loving that she couldn't help falling for him.

But here he was, her son, meeting one of the maids at the garden gates. "Jane, I think her name is, I'll have to ask Cook to be sure. But she might ask why I want to know. What would I say?"

What did he want with her and what secrets might Jane know that she could pass on? She would have to find a way of discovering the truth.

Chapter 9

Billy and Jane spent their day oblivious to Alice's secret. Billy had plucked a rose from one of the bushes as they passed, giving it to Jane and declaring that he loved her. Jane was delighted and told him she felt the same way.

"But my father is a difficult man." She advised.

"He has forbidden me to see you again, so I won't be able to introduce you to my family. We will have to continue this relationship in secret, at least for the time being."

"But surely you can lead your own life?" answered Billy "Can't your mum do anything? And he won't always have a hold over you, we'll work something out, even if we have to elope and find our own way in the world."

Jane looked at him adoringly. "Yes, I suppose." She replied. "Let's just enjoy our time together and see what happens. I love you and I don't want to lose you."

"That could never happen. I love you too and we will find a way to get married even if your dad tries to stop us."

Eventually, it was time for Jane to get back to work, so Billy escorted her back and gave her a soft kiss as he left. She stood there for a minute to catch her breath and watched him until he disappeared from sight. She drifted into the kitchen in a slight trance. She couldn't quite believe that Billy loved her as much as she loved him. But he said he did and she would just have to believe him.

Alice saw them return. Should she confront the maid and find out what he wanted from them? But what if her husband found out. Would he divorce her? Could he ever forgive her for keeping such a huge secret from him?

What should I do? She fretted.

As she was watching out of the window John returned home from his trip to London. Alice groaned. That was just what she needed. John had never liked her. His mother had died in childbirth and the nurse that had brought John up had spoiled him a great deal.

His father had been devastated by John's mother passing and had thrown himself into his work and was hardly around. Whenever he was there, John would demand his attention and because Ron felt guilty for being so immersed in his work, he had pandered to his every whim. Consequently, John had grown up expecting to be centre of attention and when Ron had met Alice and they had fallen in love, John had been very difficult to be around.

In fact, they had nearly split up because of his attitude towards Alice, but at the last minute Ron had given John a role which meant him spending most of his time in London, so persuaded Alice that John wouldn't be there to interfere in their day-to-day lives. Ron was a kind man but could be quite weak when it came to his son, so this was a bit of a breakthrough.

Things were still very tense when he was around, and she tried to avoid him as much as possible. If he were to find out her secret, there would be no way that he wouldn't use it against her.

She started to panic. *How has my son managed to find me? What is he doing here and what does he want? What if John finds out about him? I won't be able to cope.* She started to perspire heavily and decided to lie down for a time.

That's where Ron found her when he went looking for her after she hadn't arrived at the dinner table. "Are you okay, my love?" he asked her.

"Just a little under the weather." She replied.

"Oh, I hope you're not coming down with something. Should I ask Cook to prepare you a plate to eat up here?"

"That would be lovely. I'm sure I'll feel better tomorrow." She whispered.

Ron left and went downstairs to talk to Cook. Alice felt awful lying to her husband. "Though it's not really a lie, I suppose, I am feeling ill. I just didn't tell him why."

But how long can I keep this secret? Would it be better if I told him before he found out from someone else? she thought.

She felt sick with the worry and didn't know what to do for the best.

Chapter 10

It was nearly pay day again, and although Jane wanted nothing more than to visit her mum, she didn't relish the thought of seeing her dad again. If he asked about Billy, she would have to lie to him. Plus, if she was spending the day at home, she wouldn't get to see Billy that week. She felt a little selfish but was hoping that some miracle would keep her around town, so she could see him.

The Friday before she was due home, Jane received a letter from her parent's neighbour, Harry.

It said, *Good day Jane, I hope this finds you well. I just wanted to write to you to tell you that your mum seems to have disappeared. I hadn't seen her for a few days, so went around to see her, but got no answer. I tried asking your dad, but he just grunted at me. Your most humble servant, Mr Bennett.*

Jane was distraught. What was going on, where was her mother? The next couple of days went in a bit of a haze and when Sunday morning came, she was up with the larks hurrying home to find out what had happened to her mum.

She arrived and pushed open the door panting. She looked around and no one was there. As she pondered on what to do next, the door opened behind her. She swung around and her father was stood in front of her.

"Where's mum?" She asked.

"Gone!" he replied.

"Where?"

"How the hell should I know. I came home last week and she had disappeared. No sight of her at all."

"Not even a note?"

"Nothing you stupid girl. What do you think I meant by disappeared?"

"Why didn't you let me know?"

"What would you have done about it? Nothing, that's what. The same as you'll do now. So, what was the point?"

Jane wanted to tell him that if she'd known earlier, she could have started looking for her, but she was scared of his reaction if she pushed him too far.

"So, hand over your wages." He demanded

Jane passed over her wages fearfully and watched him pocket the money without as much as a thank you.

"You'll be giving me your wages from now on." He said. "Your mum's not here to do the housekeeping, so I'm going to need it."

Jane nodded reluctantly and then made her way to the door. Her dad had got what he wanted and let her go without a word. She decided to pay a visit to their neighbour to see if he had learned anything new and to thank him for letting her know her mum wasn't around.

She knocked politely and waited patiently until Harry opened the door. He gave a huge smile and invited her in. "Any news?" he asked.

"No, I was hoping you might have something." Jane replied.

"Nothing. I mean they were rowing as usual and I think he hit her, but it couldn't have been too bad, because she didn't come and knock the door, like she does sometimes.

That was news to Jane. She hadn't realised that Mary had been so friendly with their neighbour and that he had helped her when she had needed it.

"When did you last see her?" she asked.

"I'm not sure. Maybe last Sunday, or it may have been Monday."

"About a week then?"

"Yes, about that. You've got no idea where she may have gone?"

"Nothing." She replied.

She said thank you to Harry and asked him to get in touch if he heard anything and decided to head back. She wasn't sure what she thought. *Would mum have left without letting me know?* She didn't think so, but to think otherwise was to think that her dad had done something unforgivable and surely that couldn't be the case. *Could it?*

Chapter 11

J ane returned to Osbourne House frantic with worry. She didn't
    know who to turn to. She hasn't told anyone at work about her
dad beating her and her mum. She was scared that if she mentioned
anything now, they might think her dad could make an appearance at
the house and cause a scene. She didn't want anything happening that
could jeopardise her position at the House. This was her only way out
of the hellish life she had had when she was living with her father.

When Jane crept up to their room Daisy was there and noticed
straight away that something was wrong. "What is it?" she asked. "Was
everything okay at home?"

Jane broke down in tears, not being able to hide her distress. "No,
not really. My mum has disappeared and I don't know what to do."
She managed to get out in between sobs

Daisy was shocked. "What do you mean, disappeared? You don't
know where she is? Could she have gone visiting a relative and forgotten to tell you?"

"No, we have no other family. I think dad has done something
awful!"

"Why would you think that?" exclaimed Daisy.

Jane explained how her dad would regularly beat on both her and
her mum. "But mum got the worst of it. When I was little, I would
hide around the neighbour's house, and sneak back when everything

had gone quiet. When I got older it was more difficult. And then I found this job. It was like a dream come true."

Daisy was appalled. "Why haven't you told me all this before?"

"I was embarrassed." Replied Jane.

"Don't be silly. Poor you. How awful. What a nasty man your dad is."

"What should I do?" asked Jane.

"Tell Cook, she'll know what to do. Maybe Billy could put the word out too? The cotton mill industry is quite close-knit, I think."

Jane smiled at Daisy. Although she was still anxious, she felt much better about the situation. Cook would know what to do, and Jane would have to risk her position to find out what had happened to her mum. She just couldn't bear not knowing.

The next morning, she told Cook all about it and she promised Jane that she would ask around and see if anyone had heard anything. She didn't tell Jane but she decided that she would also have a quiet word with the local constabulary, see if they had any news.

After mentioning it to Cook, she decided she couldn't wait until the following Sunday to ask for his help so she sent a short note out to Billy, asking him if he could meet her outside the gate that evening. She then got on with her work with a slighter lighter heart.

Jane hated the thought of doing anything improper, but she was desperate to get wheels in motion, so at the allotted time, she crept down to the back door and snuck out. She had finished all of her chores but wasn't supposed to leave the premises during the week. "I'm not really breaking the rules. I won't leave the grounds of the house. I'll keep inside the garden gate and talk to Billy through it."

Billy was there waiting for her. "What is it?" he asked. "The note didn't say anything except to come here this evening. Is everything okay? Did your dad find out about us?"

"No nothing like that. Don't worry." Jane replied before telling him about her mum's disappearance. "Do you think there is anything you can do to find out what might have happened?"

"I don't know," responded Billy gently, "but I'll certainly try."

"Thank you. I don't know what I would do without you. I must go back. I'm not supposed to leave my quarters after hours."

Billy gave her a brief peck and said "Okay my love, until Sunday. I hope to have some news for you then."

Jane nodded and said her goodbyes and started to scurry back to her room when she bumped into John, who had seen the exchange with Billy and didn't like it one bit.

What's that hussy doing with him? he thought as he made his way over to cut her off from the house.

"Oops." Said John. "What are you doing out here? I thought you weren't supposed to leave the house?"

"Oh." Stammered Jane, who hadn't realised that John had returned home. "My mum wasn't very well when I went home the other week. I was worried, so a family friend was just bringing me the news that she was better now." She lied, not wanting him to know her business.

"He seemed quite friendly for a family friend?" responded John tartly.

"I'd better go, Sir. Cook will be looking for me." Jane said anxiously, looking at him for permission to leave.

"Well, go girl, you don't want to get yourself into trouble do you?" he said dismissively. *I'm certainly not going to chase her, but if I get a chance, who knows what might happen?* he thought as he watched her hurrying away.

Jane rushed back to the house, crept up the stairs, and softly pushed open the door. Daisy was sound asleep, so Jane quietly got ready for bed and slipped between the covers. She felt that she had done everything she could for the time being and exhausted she drifted off to sleep.

A couple of days later Daisy cornered Jane during her duties. "What have you been doing?" she hissed

"Nothing." Replied Jane worriedly. "Why?"

"I heard Master John talking about you to his parents. He was making some snide remarks about you disappearing off out at nights with some young lad, getting up to all sorts. Are you sure you haven't been up to something?"

Jane explained to Daisy about the night she had slipped out of the house to tell Billy about her mum. "I just couldn't wait until Sunday. You do understand, don't you?"

"Of course. But maybe you should tell Cook about it. At least that way, she might give you a telling-off, but that should be it. If she hears the stories and finds out you've lied to her, she might believe his lies. This way she can stick up for you with Mr and Mrs Morgan if they start saying anything."

Jane reluctantly agreed to tell Cook. "It's better if she hears it from me, rather than from some odious young man, I suppose, but I did nothing wrong. I hope she doesn't get too upset."

The next morning, she explained everything to Cook, who wasn't best pleased, but deep down understood why Jane had done such a thing. "You silly girl, you'll be getting yourself into trouble, if you're not careful. Now, I think the best thing to do would be for me to mention it to Mrs Morgan so that if Master John says anything else, she will know not to take any notice. Now go along girl, get on with your chores."

With that Jane felt relieved that there were no further consequences and went off to scrub the kitchen floors. *I better make sure that I work extra hard to make up for the inconvenience I'm causing Cook,* she thought.

On Sunday she met with Billy as usual and explained the situation with John. "How dare he." Billy fumed. "I've got a good mind to go round there and give him a piece of my mind. Spreading rumours about you, and sullying your good name."

"Don't do anything rash. I need the job and now Cook knows what I did, she has promised to have a quiet word with Mrs Morgan, so please don't say anything. You could make it worse" Jane pleaded.

Chapter 12

Billy calmed down slightly and threaded her arm between his and they started to head towards the park, as they usually did on Sundays.

"So, did you hear anything?" asked Jane. "About my mum?"

"Sorry, but no. I did hear some gossip about your dad and how he was becoming a nuisance at The Bull. Apparently, he keeps going in there, trying to cadge a drink off of the other locals. They say he's struggling to manage since your mum left. But where they think she's gone, they can't say."

Jane was so disappointed that she had to bite on her lip to stop the tears from falling. "Oh well. That's that, I suppose. Thank you anyway for asking for me."

"I'm so sorry, my love. I'm sure she'll turn up when she thinks it safe to do so and, in the meantime, you've got me and you've got Daisy and Cook looking out for you, from what you've told me."

They continued their stroll through the park. Jane was mightily disappointed but understood that Billy had done all he could. Maybe Cook will have more luck. She thought hopefully.

While they were spending the afternoon together, Alice was sat in the drawing-room quietly reading. It's a past time she'd always enjoyed and liked, even more, when John is at home. He didn't often frequent the drawing room, so she felt much more peaceful hid in there alone.

She heard a gentle tap at the door, then the maid entered. "What is it?" Alice asked.

"I've got a letter for you ma'am."

"Well place it down over there and I'll get to it shortly," Alice said dismissing the servant.

The door closed and Alice's curiosity was peaked. "How am I getting a letter now? I didn't hear anyone arrive. I wonder who it is from."

She glided across the room and picked up the letter and turned it over, looking at it in bewilderment. There was no stamp, the writing was quite bland, she certainly didn't recognise it. There was nothing more to be done, but to open it and find out who it was from and what they wanted.

She tore open the envelope and opened the folder paper and started to read the letter which said. "I know your secret." Alice paled as she continued to read. "I know all about the boy who turned up here the other day and who he is. You better tell your husband everything that happened, or I'll tell him for you. Just because the vicar is now dead, I know people who will verify my story."

Alice dropped the letter in shock. *Who has sent this letter? Was it my son and what did he want? And if it wasn't him, who else could it be and how did they find out about it all.* She wasn't sure what to do. *I don't want to tell Ron. What if he couldn't forgive me. What if he threw me out on the streets? My father certainly wouldn't take me back in, if he knew about the baby.*

There was another knock on the door. Alice bent down quickly and picked the letter up before the maid entered the room. "Are you alright ma'am. You look a little faint. Can I get you anything?" she asked as she placed the cup and saucer onto the nearby table for afternoon tea.

"I'm okay." Responded Alice quietly. "I think I may have just stood up a little quickly. Just had a small dizzy spell." she lied. "Could you please ask Cook to come up and see me?"

"Of course, ma'am." The maid replied, leaving the room.

A few minutes later, Cook appeared at the door. "You wanted to see me, ma'am?"

"Yes, Cook. I was wondering if you knew anything about this letter. Where it might have come from. Did you see anyone dropping it off?"

"No, ma'am. It just turned up on the side, and so I told the girl to bring it to you straight away, just in case it was important. But now you mention it ma'am, it is a little weird that I didn't see anyone drop it off. Would you like me to ask around?"

"No, no. It's fine." Alice replied quickly. The fewer people who knew about the letter the better. *I'll have to make some discreet enquiries but where do I even start?*

"Will that be all ma'am?" Cook said, interrupting Alice's thoughts.

"Yes, of course. Thank you." Alice said dismissing Cook and going back to her thoughts.

Cook looked at her and left the room, worrying that this kind, gentle lady might have some troubles, but knowing that it wasn't her place to pry.

Chapter 13

Jane was woken by a loud knocking at her bedroom door. *What is it?* she thought coming to. She rushed out of the bed and grabbed her clothes.

"One minute." She called out.

She looked around at Daisy, who was rubbing her eyes in bemusement. *It was too early to be up, wasn't it?* she thought

Jane answered the door to one of the stable hands. "It's your dad." He said "There's a man downstairs who says that he's had a fall. He's in a bad way."

Jane ran downstairs to the back door, where Mr Bennett was stood. "Jane, you must come quickly. Your father was drunk and he fell down the stairs. I called the doctor, but I'm not sure he's going to make it. You need to come now."

Jane panicked. If her dad died, how would she ever know what happened to her mum? She pulled on her boots and her coat and started for the door. As she was leaving Cook came down the stairs. "Where are you going child?"

"It's my dad. He's had a fall. I think he's dying. I must go." She replied.

"Okay, but get back here as soon as possible. We need you here too." Cook told her.

Harry took Jane's arm and they ran out towards the entrance, where Harry had managed to borrow a horse and cart from a nearby farmer. They trotted back to the village, where he led Jane into the house. Her father was lying on the table, with the doctor standing above him.

The doctor looked around as they entered. "I'm sorry, there was nothing I could do. He's dead."

Jane ran over to her father. He had been a mean and miserly man, but he had been the only dad she'd known. She looked at his face, looking peaceful for once and felt thankful that there was no way that he could ever hurt her again. She turned to Harry and said flatly. "Now I'll never find out what happened to mum."

Harry drew her into his arms and gave her a fatherly hug. "Leave it with me. I'll see what I can find out. That's if you want me to?" he asked gently. "Now leave all this with me and I'll make funeral arrangements and everything. You just get back to your job. You'll need it more than ever now."

His comforting words made Jane feel a little safer. Her father was gone and if her mum was still alive, maybe she'd hear the news and return to her. She thanked Harry and took a final look around what had been her home for such a long time.

It had never been a big place. Two rooms, both tiny, but mum had always kept it clean and tidy. She had taken great pride in the few possessions she'd had and made sure that they were looked after to the best of her ability. If she could see it now, it was a hovel. Dad hadn't cleaned anything since her mum's disappearance. There was a funny musty smell and even the windows were covered in a sooty substance. She would be glad to leave the place and get back to normality.

As she left, she felt that a weight had been taken off her young shoulders. She marched back to the House, not wanting to let Cook down. She had done so much for her in the short period that she had known her.

Ron was already sitting down at the dinner table when Alice arrived. She looked around and asked "No John?"

"He's out with friends for the evening. It's just you and me for dinner."

Alice smiled. She was always anxious when John was around and that feeling seemed to have intensified since his return this time. She couldn't quite put her finger on it, but she was sure he was up to something.

She sat down next to Ron. If John had been there, she would have had to sit at the other end of the long table and she always felt a bit lost there. "Are you okay my dear?" he asked. "You look a little pale?"

"I'm fine. Just tired, that's all." She replied.

"Are you sure? You seem to have been quite upset this past couple of days and there seems to be a tenseness between the two of us. Is it John?" He fretted.

"No, everything is okay, I promise." Alice hated lying but was too scared to say any more. "I'm probably just a little under the weather. I expect I'll be fine in the morning."

Ron said no more but continued to look at her worriedly all evening. Alice picked at her food, finding it difficult to swallow, feeling uncomfortable under his scrutiny. *Perhaps he already knows. Maybe he's just waiting for me to confess. What if I don't say anything and he starts to hate me for keeping it from him. What am I to do?* The worries whirred about her mind, making her feel sick to the pit of her stomach.

Chapter 14

At the end of the meal, where Alice has eaten hardly anything, Ron turned to her.

"Right, now you must tell me what's wrong. I can see you're upset and I can't help but be concerned. You've hardly eaten anything. You've been offish with me lately. Don't you love me anymore? Are you ill? You're not dying or something are you? You must tell me. I'm out of my mind with worry about what could be wrong." He pleaded

Alice sat there in shock. She hadn't realised that her demeanour had changed so much or that her worries had been so obvious. *How could he think I don't love him anymore? It's the opposite of that. Since finding that letter, I've realised how much I do love him. I'm going to have to tell him and hope against all odds that he still loves me once he's heard my story.*

She stood up from her chair and knelt in front of Ron saying, "My darling, of course, I love you. I will always love you and you must remember that when I tell you what I'm about to tell you. I'm not ill my love, but I am sick with worry that what I tell you will make you hate me and I couldn't bear it. I just couldn't." she said dramatically.

"There is nothing you could say that would make me hate you. You know how much I adore you." He replied, pulling her up into his arms. "Okay, well let's go to the drawing room, where we won't be disturbed and you can tell me what it is that's bothering you."

They rang the bell to let the servants know that it was okay to clear the dining room and Ron took Alice's arm and led her gently into the drawing room. "Please make sure we're not disturbed." He said over his shoulder to the girl clearing the table.

"Yes sir." She responded.

He closed the door to the drawing room, and they sat side by side on the floral couch close to the fireplace. He poured them both a drink and said "I'm listening."

"I don't know where to start. Shall I start right from the beginning, or should I jump to the bit that I'm most afraid to tell you? I have so much to explain and it was so long ago, and it's all so muddled in my head now. I want you to understand what I was like back then and how much I've changed."

Ron was totally confused. "My dear, what are you trying to tell me? Just start where you think best and I'll listen to it all."

"Well, okay. First, I was very young and thought I was madly in love. We were engaged to be married you see..."

"Who were? What? You were engaged before? Why didn't you tell me? Ron interrupted.

"Please Ron, can't I just tell you what happened, and then you can ask me anything you want. But if you keep interrupting, I will lose my thread and maybe miss out on an important detail. I want you to know exactly what happened back then, so there are no more secrets."

Ron agreed and Alice told him the whole story, of her young love for this man. How they had got carried away one night and soon after she had found out that she was pregnant, but not until after he had died of a sudden illness.

"I didn't know what to do." She explained. "So, a friend and I, we went away for a few months. I had the baby, but I couldn't keep it. I would have been cast out. I would never have met you, and we wouldn't be married now."

"So, what did you do?" he asked

She continued to tell him all about leaving him with a note at the church. How they had kept watch, hidden behind the trees until the vicar had arrived and taken him in. "I went back twelve months later, but he had been adopted by a young couple, and they had moved away. There was no more that I could do, so I had to put him to the back of my mind. I still think of him to this very day, wishing there was more that I could have done for him."

She realised that Ron had turned away from her slightly. "Oh Ron, my dear husband, please tell me that it doesn't make any difference to the way you feel about me. Tell me you still love me, please." She begged.

Ron turned ashen-faced. "I can't believe it. Why have you never told me this before? How have you kept something so big hidden from me?"

"Please Ron. I was scared. I didn't know what you would say. I didn't want this coming between us."

"What's changed?" he asked.

Jane explained about the letter, taking it out of her pocket and showing it to Ron. Ron took it from her hand and read it. "You would never have told me if you hadn't received this? You would have kept this secret from me forever. I feel I don't know you at all" he stormed.

"I don't know. I was so scared. Can you forgive me? Please." She pleaded.

"I don't know what to think, or how I feel at the moment." He said angrily. "I'm going to bed, and I'll have to think about what happens next."

Alice hurried after him, but he slammed the door in her face and was gone. "What have I done?" she sobbed to herself uncontrollably.

Chapter 15

The next day Jane was busy scrubbing the floors when Cook entered the kitchen and looked around at her. "What have you done?" she asked a bit sternly.

"Nothing... why?" Jane responded.

"Well, Mrs Morgan would like to see you. It was all a little mysterious if you ask me. Now, tell me, have you done something you shouldn't have?"

"No..." stuttered Jane. "Unless someone saw me in Master John's suite and she is going to rebuke me for that, but that was weeks ago."

"Aye, you could be right." Cook responded, "You better get up to the drawing room and find out what she wants."

Jane went directly up the stairs towards the drawing room, frightened that she was going to be given notice. She couldn't think of anything she had done wrong, even being in the master's quarters had been a genuine mistake on her part.

She knocked timidly at the door and was told to enter, which she did quietly. She stood with her back to the door, not knowing what to do next. She had never been upstairs, apart from that one day when she had got lost, looking for Daisy.

She looked around her in awe. The room was so grand. Nothing like it was downstairs. Everything was light and airy, with wooden panelling on the walls. There were several settees in the room, all centered around a huge fireplace with a grand golden mirror above it. There were lots of pictures on the wall and a beautiful chandelier hanging from the middle of the ceiling.

What she noticed as she was looking around her, was one of the photos. "That looks just like Billy." She gasped, drawn to it from where she was standing.

She suddenly realised where she was and turned towards Mrs Morgan. "I'm sorry ma'am. It's just that this picture looks exactly like someone I know. Who is it? Sorry ma'am, I didn't mean to be rude" Again realising that she was upstairs and really shouldn't be so impertinent.

Alice smiled at her. "That's okay. It's my baby brother when he was younger. Unfortunately, he died in the outbreak of cholera some years back. He was quite beautiful, wasn't he?"

"Yes ma'am." Jane responded. "Cook said you wanted to see me?"

"Can I swear you to secrecy?" asked Alice.

Jane was confused. What did Mrs Morgan want with her and what secret was she going to share with a lowly scullery maid? It all sounded a little odd.

"I suppose so ma'am. What is it?"

"I was wondering about the boy I saw you with the other day?" questioned Alice.

"That was Billy ma'am, the boy that looks just like this photo."

"And what do you know of him? Do you know where he was born? Was it here?"

"No, ma'am. He was adopted as a baby, and they moved here for work when he was less than a year old. What is it ma'am? Did you know his parents?"

"Sit down girl. I'm going to tell you a story and see if it matches what you know about your Billy."

Jane sat down tentatively. She was covered in grime from the scrubbing earlier that day and didn't want to get the chair dirty. Alice smiled and explained to Jane about a young girl who had got in the family way and had left their child on the steps of a church, where he had been taken in by the local vicar.

"Why, that's what happened to Billy. How did you know? Did you know his mother?"

Seeing Alice's face, Jane gasped.

"Oh! Were you the girl? Are you Billy's mum? He will be so excited to meet you, I know he will. I mean he loves his adopted parents, but you're his real mum. I can't wait to tell him."

"No." exclaimed Alice. "You can't tell him anything. That's why I swore you to secrecy. This is between you and me. I just wanted you to tell me something about the character of the boy. Is it likely that he would try to blackmail me, by telling my husband my secret?"

Jane was bewildered.

"What? No! He would never do such a thing. He is a good, honest man, he is kind and gentle and would never do something to hurt you, especially not his family."

"Well, who else knows about Billy being adopted? Does anyone in the house, someone who knows me?"

"I don't think so ma'am. I haven't told anyone. I didn't think it right that I shared his story. It's for him to tell, not me and no one has asked me about it, not that I can remember."

Alice realised that Jane didn't know anything and that maybe she had shared too much already with the girl. *After all, I don't know her, or the type of family she was brought up in. But she seems to be an honest worker and Cook has good things to say about her, so maybe she is trustworthy.*

"So, can I trust you not to say anything to anyone?" she asked Jane.

"What, not even Billy?"

"Especially not him. Remember you promised."

"What about Cook? What will I tell her? I don't like to lie." Jane asked.

"Tell her I wanted to know if you knew anything about a letter that arrived a few days ago. I'll say the same thing. Don't worry."

Alice dismissed Jane and Jane tiptoed unhappily down the stairs. She didn't like secrets, but this one wasn't hers to share, so she would do as Mrs Morgan asked and keep quiet.

After Jane left, Alice flopped back down into the settee, looking up to the ceiling. *If it wasn't Billy who wrote that letter, who was it?*

Chapter 16

Over the next few days, Jane was quite subdued and Cook was worried about her. "Are you okay? Is it your mum? Is there still no news?"

That had been playing on Jane's mind, along with everything else, so she nodded. "Yes, I'm really worried, no one seems to know anything. You didn't hear anything did you?" as she remembered that Cook had promised to ask around.

"Nothing, yet child. I'm sorry." Cook replied.

Sunday came around and it was payday. Normally Jane would go to her mums, but as she had no idea where to find her, she had arranged to meet Billy. She was a little nervous that she would let slip some detail of what had been discussed in the drawing room and was a little quiet when Billy found her waiting for him at the gate.

"Are you okay? He asked as they were walking arm and arm towards the park.

"I'm fine." Replied Jane. "Just missing my mum."

"Okay," Billy said. "I'll have to try and cheer you up then."

As they walked through the park, Billy pointed out some of the bright flowers that were appearing within the borders and nudged her as a squirrel ran in front of them. But Jane's head was far away, and she hardly seemed to notice when a butterfly landed on her knee.

"Right. There's definitely something wrong. Tell me what it is." Billy demanded.

"It's nothing." Said Jane, scared that she would say something that would give away the secret.

Billy kept trying to find out what was wrong, but the more he dug, the more Jane withdrew. "Is it that John again? Has he been pestering you? If I find out he has, I'll be right round there, telling him what's for."

"It's not John, it's nothing. Please Billy, just leave it." Jane pleaded.

"You obviously don't trust me, otherwise you would tell me what was bothering you and don't say nothing again. I know there is, so what is it?"

"It's nothing," Jane repeated forlornly.

"If you can't trust me, then we're through. Without trust, this is going nowhere. I can't live with secrets." Billy said angrily, turning away and stomping off.

"Billy, wait." Cried Jane.

Billy turned to face her and demanded "Are you going to tell me what is wrong?"

Jane faltered, then shook her head.

Billy turned and left abruptly.

Jane found the bench and sat down, sobbing. She couldn't break her promise, but how could she lose Billy? Once the tears had subsided, she decided to go to see her old neighbour, Mr Bennett. Maybe he could help. He'd always given her sound advice before. She wouldn't need to tell him the whole story, but she could give him the gist, and see what he thought she should do.

She ran most of the way, knowing that there wasn't much time before she was due back at the House. She tapped impatiently at the door and Harry opened it quickly.

"Is there a fire?" he asked

"No," said Jane confused.

"I wondered what the hurry was?" he joked, before seeing how upset Jane was. "Come in, tell me all about it, and I'll see what I can do to help you." He promised gently.

He let her in and she sat down. "So, tell me all about it," Harry said.

Jane told him as much as she could, without mentioning any names, or betraying any secrets. "Oh, dear me. What a pickle. I can see why you were in such a quandary. I suppose the young man you refer to is Billy?"

"Yes, but please don't ask me anything more. I can't tell you. I promised. I wish I hadn't. In fact, I wish I knew nothing about it at all." She said, close to tears again.

"I won't. I promise. And if Billy is half the man you say he is, he'll come around, mark my words. He'll be back, cap in hand apologising to you. Tell him you have a secret, but it's not your secret. He might not be happy, but he will understand, and maybe one day, the secret will be revealed."

Jane half-smiled, comforted by his words, but worried that he might not be right this time. She thanked him for his advice and then asked if there was any news about her mum. Harry hadn't heard anything and so, with a heavy heart, Jane said her goodbyes and made her way back to the House.

Chapter 17

A few days later, things were still a little tense around the family living quarters. John knew something was wrong between his father and Alice and was delighted. He had never approved of their marriage. He thought that Alice had been much too young for Ron and worried that if she had a baby, that he would lose some of his inheritance.

"Alice is quiet," John said to his father as they were sitting down to breakfast one morning. "Something I've said?" he asked snidely.

"It's nothing," Ron replied, not wanting to discuss the matter with John. He knew that there was no love lost between Alice and the boy and definitely didn't want to give him further ammunition in their relationship.

"But father, it feels like she's hiding something. Whatever could it be?" John asked.

"Whatever do you mean? Do you know something?" his father queried suspiciously.

"No, why? Is there anything? I bet there is. I bet she's not who she says she is or something." John surmised.

"There's nothing to tell. Now that's Alice on the stairs. Let's put an end to all this nonsense. I don't want you bothering Alice with all your rumour-mongering." Ron said hearing Alice coming down to join them.

He's right though, thought Ron, she doesn't look well. I think maybe we should talk again later. Clear the air. I don't want to lose her; I just need to decide if I can forgive her.

He smiled softly at Alice and said "Good morning my dear. Did you sleep well?"

Alice glanced over tiredly. "Good morning. Yes, thank you, but I am still weary. What about the both of you?"

John smiled inwardly. There was something amiss and he was going to do his best to make sure the situation didn't improve. *But what?* he thought furtively.

They ate breakfast mostly in uncomfortable silence. Alice didn't want to address Ron in front of John, as she was worried that he might ignore her, even though he is a perfect gentleman and I'm sure he wouldn't do that to me. She thought.

Ron was unsure how to start a conversation, while John seemed to enjoy the awkwardness and purposely did nothing to ease the tension at the breakfast table.

Even the servants had noticed that something was going on. "It's odd upstairs," Daisy whispered to Jane. "something's going on. The master is looking strangely at ma'am and she looks like a frightened rabbit most of the time. Master John seems to be enjoying it though. Nasty man that he is."

Jane didn't know what to say. She wondered if it was anything to do with the secret that Mrs Morgan had shared with her. Cook heard Daisy gossiping and said sternly "Now young'uns, you stop that chattering, nothing good will come of it, and anyway, Jane don't you have some floors to scrub?"

Jane nodded and scurried off thankful for Cook's interruption. She didn't want there to be any risk that she would accidentally slip something out. *No. Best to keep out of it.* She thought as she bent to her knees with the scrubbing brush and a bucket of soapy water in hand.

Alice heard a knock at the door and said "Come." Expecting one of the servants to enter. Instead, Ron appeared.

"Have you got a minute or two?" he asked.

"Of course." She replied. "I've always got time for you." She put down her needlework and turned towards him, giving him her full attention.

Ron sat down and said "It's about the matter we discussed the other day. I just wanted to tell you I've thought about it. I don't fully understand how it came about and all the reasons you had for keeping it from me. But I love you and if you have a son, then I should love him too. What do you know about him? Does he seem to be a decent lad? Maybe we should invite him around and get to know him?"

Alice was shocked. She'd hoped that Ron would forgive her, but she never thought she would get the chance to meet her son and to invite him into their lives. "Are you sure my love? It seems a lot to ask of you."

"I'd do anything for you. You know I would." Ron replied tenderly.

"And I you." Alice said. "But how can we invite him around? He doesn't even know who I am. He's never even seen me."

"Okay, we'll invite him around and can tell him who you are to him, together. Then we can get to know him and discuss what to do next, once we've met him and ascertained his character."

As they continued their discussions, Ron started to warm to the idea. After all, Alice wasn't the mother of John, so what was the difference? Anyway, it might do John good to have another youngster in the house. He had been a little spoiled over the years.

What they hadn't realised was that John had been standing outside the door and had heard snippets of the conversation. He was furious.

How dare they think they could do anything to jeopardise his future by bringing this pretender in? "I'm going to put a stop to this one way or another." He promised himself.

Chapter 18

When Billy returned home from work dirty and tired, he was confused to see his mum standing there with a letter in her hand for him.

"What's that?" he asked.

"How should I know?" she responded. "But it looks a bit posh. Open it and find out who sent it and what they want."

Billy took the envelope and turned it over in his rough hands. He lifted it to his nose. It had a gentle scent of flowers. He'd never received a letter before and was bemused. "Open it!" his mother said impatiently.

He turned it back over and used his pocket knife to slit open the envelope and read its contents. "Who's it from? What do they want?" she asked anxiously. "Is it bad news?"

He turned to her perplexed. "It's from the couple who own the house that Jane works in. They want me to visit tomorrow, just after lunch. What could they want?"

"Maybe it's something to do with Jane?" She suggested.

"Maybe," he replied. "but what would they want from me and how do they know where I live?"

Billy had more questions than answers and his mum couldn't be of any help. "You'll just have to wait until tomorrow and find out." She said finally.

He hardly slept at all that night, with all the questions whirling about his brain. "I hope that Jane is not ill. I want to tell her I'm sorry and ask for her forgiveness. I don't care what she's keeping from me, as long as she loves me."

The next morning, he was grateful that it was the weekend and he wouldn't have to be operating machinery when he was so tired. He had a good wash and put on his best clothes and made his way to the house. He got there dead on the allotted time and knocked on the servant's entrance. He was hoping that Jane would answer the door and he would have time to make sure she was okay, before going upstairs.

But it was Cook that opened the door and looked at him sternly. "Hello, who are you and what do you want?"

Billy showed her the letter and perplexed, Cook let him enter the home. "Wait there, lad. I'll go and speak with Mrs Morgan and see where she wants you. Don't you be stealing anything when my back's turned mind."

"Yes, ma'am. I won't ma'am." He stammered.

"I'm Cook, not ma'am." She told him, smiling as she did so. *He seems a polite young boy, But what did them upstairs want with him?* she thought, rushing upstairs to let them know he had arrived.

Coming back downstairs, she called him to her. "Come now boy, you're to come this way. They're in the drawing room and expecting you, apparently."

Billy followed her as she turned and went back up the stairs and down a long hallway. His eyes took in all his surroundings. He couldn't believe how different the house was. There were pictures everywhere, and carpeting on the floor. The picture frames were gold, he had never known such opulence. And *it's not even a room!* he thought dazed at his even being there.

Cook knocked at the door and entered as she heard the voice calling her in. "Come on boy. Look lively" She said, pulling him into the room.

Alice and Ron were sat together on a sofa near the fire. "Could you arrange tea, please Cook?" Ron asked.

"Of course, sir, right away." She said turning and leaving Billy in the room with the couple.

"Please sit down. Billy, isn't it?" Ron said gently.

Billy moved across the room and sat down in the chair that Ron had pointed towards.

Ron cleared his throat. "I expect you're wondering why you're here?" he asked Billy once he had gotten comfortable.

"Yes sir." Stammered Billy.

As Ron went to continue, there was a knock at the door and a maid entered carrying a tray with the requested tea upon. Billy looked around him, afraid that he would wake up and find that he was dreaming. He pinched his wrist, "No, not a dream." He anxiously waited, while Alice dismissed the maid and poured the tea, passing him a cup and saucer.

What on earth am I doing here? he thought.

Chapter 19

Ron coughed again. "Well young man. We've got some news for you and we thought that it would be best to do it together."

He turned to Alice and said, "Do you want to explain?"

Alice nodded nervously and blurted out, "Billy, I'm your mother."

Billy looked at her stunned. "What do you mean?"

Alice told him the story of her and his father, how her betrothed had died and she had left him at the church. "I had no choice. I had no way of looking after you and I would have been disinherited. It was for the best."

Billy sat there shocked. Everything she was telling him was true, but it made no sense. "I always knew I was adopted, my parents told me at a very young age, but to think I'm from all this!" he gestured around the room. "I can't quite take it all in."

"Take your time, son." Said Ron. "It's a lot for all of us. I've only just found out about it myself."

"I tried to find you, but when I went back, the vicar said that you and your family had disappeared. It's only when I saw you with Jane that I knew you were my son." Alice said weeping. "I'm so sorry for abandoning you."

"But how did you know I was your son?" Billy asked.

Alice walked over to the photo of her brother and brought it back to show Billy. You are the spit of my brother, so I spoke with Jane and she confirmed everything I knew."

"She never said." Billy stammered.

"I swore her to secrecy. I made her promise not to say anything to you. She wasn't happy about it, but finally, she agreed she would keep my secret."

Billy then understood why she had been so reticent at their last meeting. She had wanted to tell him and he had gotten angry with her. *I have to see her and ask her to forgive me.* He thought.

They sat there for another hour, Alice wanted to know everything about him and Billy was the same. Ron sometimes participated in the conversation, but he was mostly content watching them grow closer. He was glad that he had forgiven her for not telling him the truth at first.

Eventually, the conversation dried and Ron turned to Billy and said "So, what next?"

"What do you mean sir?" he replied

"Well, you're Alice's son, so you have a right to live here if you like? You certainly can't continue working at the cotton mill. It just wouldn't be right. There are lots of decisions to be made, but I think maybe we need to leave it for a few days. Let you tell your parents and get used to the news. Perhaps we could reconvene this time next week?"

"Reconvene?" asked Billy.

"For you to come back and for us to think about the future?"

"Oh yes, of course, sir," Billy said still shocked by the news.

Alice led him out and took him back downstairs to Cook. "My son." She said happily. "My son. I can't believe I found you again. I'm overjoyed."

Billy looked at her. "Yes, I'm happy too... I think. It's a lot to get my head around. I can't wait to tell Jane that I know. She'll be so relieved."

Alice smiled. "That she will be. I'm so sorry if I caused any rift between the two of you. I was just scared of the consequences. But I'm glad I told Ron all about you. Now we can get to know each other properly."

She left Billy with Cook, who took him into the kitchen to find Jane. Once there, he apologised to Jane, telling her he would never be angry with her again and begging her for her forgiveness. He explained what had just happened and said "I just can't believe it. It feels like a fairy tale."

Jane was ecstatic about the news. "I'm so sorry I didn't tell you, but I couldn't. I promised and I couldn't break that promise. I'm so happy that she told you and that we don't have to keep secrets from each other."

"Let's never keep a secret from each other ever again." Smiled Billy, "The one thing I am sure about, in all of this is that I love you and I want to marry you. Please say yes."

Jane jumped for joy. "I love you. Of course, I'll marry you."

Chapter 20

B illy left, and it being Sunday the next day they made arrangements to meet again at eleven o'clock to discuss the wedding
arrangements and for Jane to meet his adopted parents. Jane rushed
off to share her news with Cook and Daisy. She was so happy that Billy
had forgiven her and that the secret had been exposed. Everything was
perfect.

Cook and Daisy were delighted.

"It's just a shame that my mum isn't around to see this day." Said
Jane feeling quite forlorn.

"Well, do you have anyone else to be with you on your wedding
day?" asked Cook. "It would be a shame if you had no one to share it
with."

"Apart from you two, the one other person I'd like to be there is my
old neighbour, Mr Bennett. He's always been so kind to me. He took
me in when I needed it and he was the one who taught me to read and
write. I must let him know, oh, but when?"

She had arranged to meet Billy the next day and she couldn't miss
that. It was an important day. She was going to meet his parents for
the first time.

"I'll tell you what. Why not go now? You've nearly finished your
chores and Daisy can help out, can't you?" Cook said looking at Daisy,
who nodded in agreement.

"Oh, okay. Thank you Cook and thank you, Daisy. I'll make it up to you both, I promise."

Jane hurried off to Harry's house and excitedly knocked at the door. Harry opened it "Oh, it must be good news, you are full of smiles. Not like last time." He said winking at her.

She followed him in and said "Guess what? Billy has asked me to marry him and I've said yes. You will be there won't you?"

"Why of course. I wouldn't miss it for the world. How did this come to pass?" he asked. "Last time we spoke he had run off in anger."

Jane told him the whole story, leaving nothing out. After all, everyone would know soon enough. "Wow. What a turnaround for Billy and you, my dear. I wish you all the best." Harry smiled.

Jane looked at him tenderly. He had always looked out for her and she knew he was genuinely pleased for her. He was much more of a father figure than her dad had ever been. "In fact, Mr Bennett would you please do me the honour of giving me away?" she asked hesitantly.

Harry was delighted. "Why of course I would. Nothing would give me greater pleasure. But if I'm to be giving you away, don't you think you should start calling me Harry, rather than Mr Bennett?"

Jane smiled and said "Thank you Mr... I mean Harry. Well, I better get back before it gets too dark. I just wanted to let you know as soon as possible."

They said their goodbyes and Jane was soon back on the road towards the House.

John had seen Billy leaving the drawing room with Cook after speaking with his father and Alice. He watched with interest, sure that he was the one that John had also seen talking with Jane.

Ron stepped out of the drawing room and saw John standing there looking down the stairs. "Oh good. Just the man I wanted to see. Would you mind coming in here for a minute? We have some news."

John followed him in and Ron shut the door and sat down next to Alice. "Why don't you sit down?" Ron said.

"I'm okay stood here." Replied John standing in front of the fire.

"Whatever you prefer," Ron said. "but you may want to sit down when we've told you what we have to say."

John reluctantly sat down and Ron explained the whole story, including the fact that they had found her son, and that it had been Billy. The man that had just left the room. The only thing he left out was about the blackmailer. It wasn't important and actually, Ron had mostly forgotten that the letter was the thing that had set the wheels in motion.

John listened with a polite look upon his face. In reality, he was furious. That woman had come here and ruined his relationship with his dad and now she dared to invite her illegitimate child here. He would never forgive her.

When his father finished telling him the story, Ron asked "So do you have any questions?"

"What is to become of her son?"

"Well, we will give him a home. Either here with us, or we will set him up in one of our smaller houses. It depends on what he wants. I believe he would like to get married, so he might prefer to start his wedded life alone with his new wife. Do you have a problem with any of that?"

John didn't want to let on how angry he was. Not before he had time to think through the consequences and so said "No father. None at all. Now, I must take my leave. I have lots of matters to deal with."

He swiftly left the room thinking, *how dare he. Who does he think he is? Coming in here, taking things that rightly belong to me. I won't have it. And that maid. She won't be getting the better of me, she better be careful.*

Ron and Alice exchanged looks. "So?" asked Ron.

"He seems to have dealt with it quite well. Who knows, maybe they'll become friends?"

Ron smiled "Let's hope so." He replied, not believing that John had taken it as well as Alice thought he had.

Chapter 21

T he next few days John was still furious and stomped around the house. The servants tried to keep out of his way. He was quite mean and vindictive when he was in a bad mood, so it was best not to give him any excuse to be nasty.

Jane was still on cloud nine. She met Billy's parents for Sunday lunch and they had got on really well. They thought that she was a sweet girl and were happy that Billy had met her. Jane had loved them from the moment she'd met them. They obviously loved Billy but were so supportive and happy that he had found his birth mother.

Jane felt slightly envious of the relationship that Billy had with his father, but she knew it was silly and did her best to shake it off, saying to Billy "It's just I've never known a father like him. Mine was the opposite in nearly every single way."

Billy smiled and told her that she could share his dad, "Now that we're to be married, dad will treat you like one of his own anyway."

Daisy had been feeling a little ill, so Jane offered to do some of her chores, to say thank you for covering her when she had gone to see Harry. With her head in the clouds, Jane didn't notice John until he was nearly on top of her.

"Oh, sorry sir." She said.

"You will be," John replied. "now come here and show me how sorry you are." He grabbed her hair and started to drag her towards him.

Jane shrieked. "Please sir, don't." she pleaded.

But John was incensed and pulled her closer into his arms, with such a strong grip that she couldn't break free. She turned her cheek. She could feel his hot breath on her and feared for what was to come.

"Please, I'm to be married." She cried, hoping to appeal to his better nature.

"And to that man!" John said through gritted teeth. "Well, he'll have to have second-hand goods. It's all he deserves anyway."

John continued to maul her, trying to push her dress from her shoulders and force his leg between hers to open them up. She was petrified. What was he trying to do?

Jane and her mother had never talked about relations between a man and a woman, and although she wasn't completely clueless, Jane was quite naïve in terms of how to deal with this situation.

"Get off me." She sobbed.

But there was no way of stopping John. He was too enraged and she could feel his sweaty hands all over her bare skin. She closed her eyes, not wanting to know what was going to happen next.

Suddenly she found herself freed. John had moved away from her. She breathed a sigh of relief and opened her eyes. There in front of her was Ron, pinning John against the wall.

"Sir, I'm sorry sir. It wasn't my fault." She begged, thinking that she would get in trouble and maybe even lose her job.

"Don't worry girl." Ron said kindly. "Go back downstairs and ask Cook to make you a hot and strong cup of tea. I'll deal with my son."

Jane pulled her sleeves up over her shoulders and hurried off, not wanting to look at the scene a minute longer. She told Cook what had happened and how Ron had saved her. "Oh child, it seems you have had a lucky escape. Go sit there, girl. I'll get that cup of tea. Put lots of sugar in it for you, for the shock."

Jane started to calm slightly and the sobs slowly stopped. "I won't get into trouble, will I?"

"Of course not. This was not down to you. It's all Master John's fault. I'm sure Sir will be dealing with him as we speak."

And Cook was right. Back up in the hallway, Ron was giving John a piece of his mind. "How dare you do that here? Do you have no respect for me or Alice? A decent human being would never even think of doing something like that. What do you have to say for yourself?" He ranted.

John looked at him with contempt. "They're just servants." He spat at his father.

"Just servants?" Ron spluttered. "I can't believe I've brought up someone like you. Now get out of my sight and if I see you treating anyone like that again, I will cut you off without a penny. Do you hear me?"

John was surprised. His father had never spoken to him like that before, but then he had never caught him with a servant before. Not that it hadn't happened, just that his father hadn't caught them. He turned, storming off and Ron slumped to the floor with his head in his hands. *How did it come to this?* he thought in despair.

Chapter 22

The next day Jane was worried that there would be repercussions and hadn't wanted to leave the kitchen, where she was under the watchful eye of Cook. She was thrilled when Daisy came downstairs and whispered to her that Master John had left the House and that no one had any idea of when he might return.

Billy had been to the house to meet with Alice and Ron a few times. They were delighted with the news that they were to be wed. "But why is she still working downstairs as a scullery maid?" Alice asked Billy during one of his visits.

"She's quite independent and wants to keep her job, at least until we get married." He explained.

Knowing this made Alice even more fond of Jane than she already had been. "I admire her character." She replied.

They had discussed Billy and Jane's living arrangements for after the wedding and they had agreed that they would move to one of Ron and Alice's smaller homes near the edge of town. It had been Ron's aunts and she had left it to him when she passed away a few years ago. "It's not quite so grand as here, but I'm sure you'll be more than comfortable there," Alice said.

When Billy had seen it, he had been astounded. Alice was right. It wasn't quite as grand as Osbourne House, but it wasn't far off. He and Jane would be rattling around it. Both Alice and Jane had thought it a wonderful idea when Billy had suggested that his adoptive parents move into one of the cottages in the grounds.

It was only a few weeks until the wedding, so Jane asked Cook if she might have a half-day to go shopping for her dress. Cook was agreeable, so Jane met Billy's mum, and they disappeared to the shops for an afternoon's outing.

She returned a few hours later with a couple of bags, one containing her wedding dress. "Come on then girl. Give us a whirl" smiled Cook.

Jane ran to her room and quickly changed into it. It was a simple styled dress, but suited Jane perfectly. "Oh, you look beautiful." Said Cook, wiping a stray tear from her eye. "And wait, us kitchen staff have clubbed together and brought you this."

She gave Jane a small box, which she opened excitedly. On seeing a small brooch inside she exclaimed delightedly "Oh, it's beautiful. It will go perfectly with this dress. Thank you Cook, thank you all. I will miss you when I leave."

"Oh, get on with you lass." Said Cook, knowing that she would also miss Jane when she was gone. "Now go and get out of that dress and back into your uniform, before you drop something on it."

Jane danced out of the room laughing and went to change back into her normal attire. When she returned to the kitchen, Cook said "ma'am wants to see you."

"What for, I wonder?" asked Jane.

"No idea, but you better look sharpish." Replied Cook

Jane went quickly up the stairs and knocked on the door. Alice called her in and asked her to sit with her for a minute. "Now, I'd like to give you something to welcome you into our family. I wasn't sure what to give you, but this is something that my mum gave to me on my wedding day and I will never have a daughter to pass it on to. You will be like my daughter, once you are married to Billy, so I want you to have it." She passed over an open box with a beautiful pearl necklace inside to Jane.

Jane gasped "But ma'am, I couldn't possibly accept this, it's too much."

"Nonsense, you must accept it. It is my gift to you." Alice smiled.

Jane graciously accepted the gift, not knowing how to thank her for such generosity and took it downstairs to show Cook. "My goodness, what a lucky young lady you are." Smiled Cook, "Couldn't happen to a nicer girl, in my opinion."

Jane looked embarrassed. She wasn't used to many compliments, especially since her mum had disappeared. She asked Cook to keep it safe for her until the wedding day and then went to bed, exhausted from all the emotions she was feeling.

I am the luckiest person alive. She thought as she drifted off to sleep.

Chapter 23

J ane woke early with a start. Today was her wedding day, she was so
   excited. She looked outside and was delighted to see that the sky
was already the most vibrant blue and the sun shining brightly as it
peered its head above the skyline. She felt a little sad, this would be her
last morning waking up in this room with Daisy. She would miss her
terribly, but she also was looking forward to setting up her own home
with Billy..

Daisy had already been up a couple of hours, trying to get as many
as her chores done as possible, so she could take a couple of hours off to
attend the wedding, so Jane had the room to herself to reflect on how
life had changed over the past nine months. "I miss my mum so much.
I wish she could be here today. I wish I knew what had happened to
her."

It soon became time for her to get ready. She scrubbed all the
residual grime from her hands and knees. She wouldn't need to worry
about that in the future. She put on her dress, pinned the dainty
brooch to her chest and went downstairs to retrieve her beautiful pearl
necklace from Cook.

Cook gasped in delight "Oh my, you look as pretty as a picture."
She said. "I'll just fetch your necklace." She turned and said, "So is Mr
Bennett collecting you from here, or meeting you at the church?"

"He'll be here any minute," Jane replied waiting for Cook to return.

"And we'll meet you there." Said Cook as she handed Jane the necklace. "As Sir and Ma'am will be at the wedding, they do not need supper this evening, so I've got permission to come for a few hours, along with Daisy."

Jane squealed with joy. "Oh, I'm so glad you can come too. It means the world to me, especially I won't have any family there with me."

"We're like your family now." Said Cook smiling.

"And we'd better get off. We don't want to be late for your wedding. We'll see you there."

As Jane was struggling with the clasp, Harry appeared with a soft tap at the door. "Can I help you with that?" he asked.

Jane turned around thankfully and Harry took the two ends from her fingers and fastened the necklace. He had managed to borrow a horse and trap from a neighbouring farmer for the day, so he helped Jane climb aboard and they made their way to the church where Billy and both lots of his parents were already waiting.

Jane went into the vestry to wait for Daisy and Cook to arrive. There were butterflies in her stomach and she could feel herself trembling all over. "Are you okay?" asked Harry.

"What if I'm making a mistake?" she asked him.

"It's normal to feel nervous. Do you love him?"

"Yes, I think so. No. I'm sure. Yes, I do love him."

"There you go then. How could you possibly be making a mistake? Everything will be fine and you'll be a married woman in no time at all." He smiled down at her

Jane smiled, the nerves starting to dissipate. She saw Daisy and Cook enter the church and waved to them as they went in and took their seats.

"Are you ready?" asked Harry.

"I suppose so." She replied, the nerves threatening to put in another appearance.

He took her arm and tucked it into his and said "Come on then. Let's go and meet your future husband."

They walked slowly down the aisle and the guests turned to watch. "Doesn't she look stunning?" She heard someone whispering as she walked past them.

She was shocked, *I would never have said I was stunning.* She thought as she reached the spot Billy was waiting for her.

He turned to her and smiled gently.

She looked at him, eyes sparkling. Here was the man she was going to marry. The nerves disappeared completely and she felt a sudden calmness envelope her. It was a perfect day and she couldn't have felt happier.

She heard the door as it squeaked open and someone crept in and sat at the back. In the darkness, Jane couldn't see who it was, but no one was going to spoil this day for her. They said their vows and the vicar pronounced them man and wife. Billy gave her a gentle kiss and they looked around. Everyone was smiling, pleased that this young couple had just joined themselves together in a new life.

Jane looked up to the character at the back of the room. Her eyes became accustomed to the light and she could see it was a woman. She was curious and as they walked out of the church, she kept her eye on the shadowy figure. "Oh my!" she said, stopping suddenly.

It was Mary. She broke free from Billy and ran over to her mum. "Where have you been, what have you been doing, why didn't you tell me where you were?"

Jane spat out a thousand questions, giving her mum no time to respond. "Hush child." Her mum said quietly. "All in good time. Just know that I would never have let you get married without me being here."

Billy came over and Jane introduced her mum and her husband to each other. "I'm so glad you could come." Said Billy. "We would have told you, but we didn't know where to find you, or if you were indeed even still alive."

Mary looked shocked, turning to Jane. "You thought I was dead? Never. Didn't you get the note I left for you?"

"No. What note?" Jane responded bewilderedly.

"I left a note in the jar in the kitchen. I knew you would go there when you next visited. If it wasn't there, your father must have found it and hidden it. He was a nasty, vindicate devil, but I can't believe he would let you think that I was dead. I hope he rots in hell!"

They continued their discussions as they went to the Inn where Ron had arranged a small gathering and some food to celebrate the marriage. Mary had finally snapped, when Fred had nearly strangled her. She had left because she thought that maybe next time, he would kill her. She had travelled quite far away and had told no one, thinking that Jane would find the letter and know that she was safe.

Finally, word got to her that the cook where Jane was working had been looking for her and she had made some enquiries, found out about the death of her husband and found out about the wedding just yesterday. "I travelled through the night to get here." She explained.

Jane and Billy shared their news with her. "Oh, my goodness. I can't believe it. You won't have to struggle your whole life, like I did. I am so happy for you both." She said, sincerely pleased that her daughter had done so well for herself.

Billy and Jane mingled with the guests, making sure that everyone was happy. Jane looked over on several occasions at her mum and each time saw her deep in conversation with Harry. She smiled. Harry was a lovely man and it was good that her mum had a friendly face there, when she didn't know anyone else.

Finally, it was time for the party to finish. Daisy and Cook had left some time earlier to make sure everything was well at the House. They had told her how lovely the day had been and to make sure she knew she was always welcome in the kitchen if she needed them. "Not that I expect you will." Said Cook. "You won't want to know us now you have that beautiful house and husband to take care of you."

"Don't even joke about it." Jane scolded. "As you said, we're family. I'll nip in soon to see you. I'm going to miss you."

Everyone else started drifting off and Billy and Jane took a stroll in the warm summer's evening towards their new home. When they arrived, they found that Alice had arranged for a few of the servants to come over and ready the house for their arrival. "She is just so lovely." Exclaimed Jane.

"We will have to go and thank them tomorrow." Replied Billy. "But now, I'm tired. Let's go upstairs."

Jane was quite nervous as she walked up the stairs behind him, but she trusted him completely and knew that he would be gentle with her.

Chapter 24

Jane woke to hear the birds singing outside their window. Last night had been magical. Nothing could have prepared her for such a wonderful night. She felt as light as feather and danced around the room singing her favourite tune.

Billy watched her from the bed. He couldn't believe he'd been so lucky. The house was beautiful and he was here with his gorgeous bride. "Are you happy my love?" he asked.

Jane bounced over to him "Of course, I've never felt happier." Then she remembered something that she hadn't yet shared with Billy and flopped onto the bed, her good mood getting overtaken with the horrible memories of that afternoon.

"What is it?" Billy asked anxiously. "You were so happy one minute and now... you look like you regret marrying me."

"It's not that." Exclaimed Jane. "It's just that I've got something to tell you and I'm not sure how you will take it, but I know you don't like secrets and neither do I."

"You can tell me anything. I promise to listen to you and then we can discuss whatever it is that you've got to tell me."

Jane was nervous but knew she had to tell Billy about the day that John had grabbed her. "He did what!" Billy's voice raised.

"You said you would hear me out." Jane responded.

"I'm so sorry I let it happen. I didn't know what to do. I couldn't stop him. Please forgive me." She pleaded.

"There's nothing to forgive you for," Billy said placatingly. "but if I ever see that monster again... I won't be held responsible for my actions."

Jane felt relieved. She had no secrets left. Billy knew everything there was to know. "Promise me, we'll have no secrets from each other." She begged.

"Don't worry. I will always tell you everything." Billy promised.

After breakfast, they decided to walk over to the House to say thank you to Alice. Jane knew that John wasn't there, so she wasn't worried that they would bump into each other. "Before we go in to see them, could we just pop our head into the kitchen? Cook has been so good to me, especially helping me find my mum. I just wanted to thank her again."

Billy agreed and they sneaked around the back to say hello. Cook was thrilled to see them. "What a great party it was." She said. "Thank you for letting me share your day with you."

"Don't be silly. Thank you for coming and sharing it with me." Jane said and hugged Cook.

"So, you're off upstairs?" Cook asked. "I'll make some tea and bring it up. Daisy, will you show them up to the drawing-room."

Daisy looked around and grinned. "Yes Cook, I'll be happy to." She wiped her hands on her apron and said "Come this way."

Jane laughed. "No need to be formal with us Daisy."

Daisy couldn't help wittering on to Jane and Billy as she showed them upstairs. She was so excited that her friend was so obviously happy. She knocked on the door and as she showed them in, she whispered "See you then."

Jane smiled and said "Bye." Then turned to greet Alice and Ron.

"Thank you so much for your generosity," Billy said to them both.

"Yes, the house is beautiful," Jane exclaimed.

Alice and Ron smiled. "It's the least we can do for you. We're family now, never forget that. Is there anything else you need?"

Billy said "No. You've already done so much. but thank you." and they sat down and talked about the day before and how it had been such a lovely day. The hours flew by and Alice suggested they stay for lunch, but Jane had promised to go and see her mum, so they politely refused and left, after arranging to come again in a few days.

As they left the grounds, Billy asked "Do you need me there with you at your mums? If not, I'd like to go and see my mum and dad. Talk to them about the moving arrangements."

"That's fine." Replied Jane. "We'll have loads to catch up on and you don't want to sit there all afternoon. I'll see you back at the house later."

They kissed tenderly and then went their separate ways.

Chapter 25

J ane made her way back to her home village and knocked on the door of her mum's home and pushed the door open. Luckily it had been standing empty, so the landlord had been happy enough for Mary to take up her lodgings again. She was surprised to see Harry sat next to her mum looking quite cosy. "Oh, hello. I wasn't expecting to see you again, quite so soon." She said.

"Harry just popped round for a cup of tea and a catch-up." Mary responded defensively. "Nothing wrong in that, is there dear?"

"Of course not, mum. I was just surprised that's all. Sorry, Harry. It's lovely to see you."

Harry looked a little guilty. "Yes, you too Jane. I suppose I'd better go. Leave you and your mum to talk."

Jane looked at him hopefully. She liked Harry but did want to spend some quality time alone with her mum.

"That's not necessary, is it Jane? Harry is welcome here, isn't he?" Mary asked.

Jane was a little confused. She thought that her mum would have been happy to see her too and would want to talk privately, but she nodded and said "Course he is. Always."

Mary nervously flitted towards the kettle to pour some more tea. "Besides," she started. "we have some news, that maybe we should share with you. Now that your dad is no longer with us."

Jane sat down and looked at them both bewildered. "What was going on? What could they possibly need to tell me, that they couldn't tell me before dad died?"

"So?" she asked.

Mary sat down wringing her hands. Where to start? she asked herself.

"Shall I tell her, or will you?" she turned to Harry.

Harry wrinkled his eyes into a soft smile. "I'll start and you can join in if I get something wrong."

He turned to Jane and said "Do you remember you always used to hide at mine when you were young? I always looked after you until your mum came to collect you?"

"Yes," said Jane, not understanding what this had to do with anything.

"Well, your mum and I have known each other for a long time. Your parents moved in next door not long after they got married. Your dad was always shouting and so I started looking out for your mum, when she left the house, just to make sure she was okay, you understand?"

Jane nodded, still not knowing what the point of the story was.

"We became quite friendly" Harry continued. "and one day after a particularly bad argument, your mum showed up on my doorstep with a split lip and a black eye."

"That was the first time your dad had ever hit me," Mary interjected.

"I invited your mum in to take refuge until your dad calmed down. I was comforting your mum when one thing led to another and we made love. It was just the once. I promise."

"All right, but why are you telling me all this?" Jane asked, thinking she might know, but feeling unsure of herself.

Mary took Jane's hands in her own and continued the story.

"A few weeks later I found out I was pregnant and I knew straight away that Harry was the father. Then eight months after that I gave birth to you. Luckily, you looked just like me, so there was no gossip or rumour-mongering."

"How do you know it was his baby, not dad's?" Jane asked "Are you sure? Did dad know? Is that why he was always so mean?"

"I just knew." Replied Mary. "Me and your dad, well the man you call dad, we never really had much of a relationship. Your dad was always too drunk. I don't know if he knew, I think he suspected, but whether he knew for sure, I don't know. I do know the beatings got worse, once you were born, so maybe he did."

Jane was dazed. She thought that she and Billy had finished with the secrets, and now, here was another one. "How would he take it. Would he be able to forgive her, just one more secret?"

"I've got to go." She said, pulling her hands from her mum and pushing herself off of the chair.

"Wait, please." Her mum pleaded, but Jane was already shutting the door behind her.

She ran through the town, not knowing where she was going or what she was doing. *What will Billy say? How am I going to break this to him? What if he hates me?*

Chapter 26

Finally, Jane ran out of steam and found herself on the road to Osbourne House. *I'll speak with Cook*, she thought. *She'll know what to do.*

She continued walking to the house, deep in thought, when she heard a familiar voice. "Oh, it's you."

It was John, she hadn't realised that he was back. She turned to hurry off, but he grabbed her arm. "Oh, no you don't." We're going to spend some time together. After all, we're family now and you know what they say about family. It's good to share things. I'm sure my dear brother won't mind." He said sarcastically.

Jane tried to wriggle out of his grasp, but he was too strong. She tried to scream, but he realised what she was doing and put one hand over her mouth. "Oh no, you don't." He said through gritted teeth. "You're coming with me."

***

Billy had not been home long. He had had a lovely time with his parents and they had arranged to move them into the small nearby cottage later that week. He couldn't wait to share his news with Jane.

It was getting a bit late, and Jane still hadn't arrived back home. Billy started to become worried. "She can't still be at her mum's, can she?"

He decided to go over to see Mary and walk Jane back if she was still there. When he got to Mary's, he found her in tears and Harry comforting her. "What's happened? Where's Jane?"

Harry retold the story of how he'd met Mary, to Jane being his daughter. Billy was shocked, but said "But where is Jane? Why didn't she come back and tell me? She knows she could tell me anything. We're husband and wife now."

He sat down with one hand pinching his forehead, trying to figure out where she might have gone. Suddenly he realised that she would have been worried about telling him. They had agreed only that morning that they had no more secrets. "I expect she's gone to see Cook and ask her advice." He said feeling relieved.

He left Mary with Harry and promised to let them know when he found Jane. He rushed off up the road leading towards the House. He was just entering the grounds when he heard a sob. "Who's that?" he called out.

Not hearing any response, he decided to go and investigate. He found Jane, dress ripped, and John gripping her tightly. "Let go of her now!" Billy shouted.

"I thought we could share, dear brother." John taunted.

"Let go of her, or I swear I'll kill you."

Jane writhed in John's arms and with him distracted, she managed to break free and ran into Billy's arms sobbing. "I thought he was going to…" she couldn't say what she thought he was going to do; it was too horrific.

"I know my love. Don't worry, I'm here and I'll deal with this." Billy said confidently.

They had been making such a racket, that the whole household knew something was going on. Ron came out with his gun. "What's going on?" he demanded, seeing the trio standing in the bushes.

"It's him." Billy said pointing at John. "He's just been manhandling my wife. He's a monster."

Ron turned to John, "Is this true? I can see it is. How dare you. This is your sister-in-law. You've got some explaining and apologising to do. To Jane, to Billy and to Alice!"

"You've never cared about me, not since that floozy came along, with her dirty little secret. You would never have found out about it either if it hadn't been for me."

"What do you mean? Was it you who sent the letter blackmailing her?" Ron asked

"It was all she deserved. She had done wrong. She needed to be found out. You should have thrown her out as soon as she told you. But no, she's got her claws into you and she can do no wrong. She'll hurt you badly one of these days and I won't be here to save you from her." John spluttered in a rage.

"Get out!" roared Ron. "You've been nothing but trouble from the day you were born. I don't know where you got such nastiness from. Your mum was a kind and generous person and Alice has been nothing but loving to you since she's been in this family. You are the one who has hurt me. Now get out and never come back."

John looked shocked. His father had always been soft and easy to, but he could see that he had pushed him too far and that his dad would never forgive him. He looked around at everyone and before marching off, said "You deserve each other. I'm off and don't worry, I won't be coming back."

Billy pulled Jane closer. "Are you okay?"

"Yes," she sobbed, "but I've got something to tell you. It's about my dad. I'm not sure if you'll be angry, but we promised no more secrets."

"I know. I've seen your mum. That's why I was coming here. I knew you would go to see Cook. I wanted to tell you it doesn't matter who your dad is. Harry seems a decent man and better than the one you thought you had, so be happy."

Turning to Ron he said "I'm so sorry that this has happened. We'll come and see you in a day or two, but I think I had better get Jane back home and let her lie down."

"Of course, dear chap and it's not you who should be apologising, it's me. If it weren't for my son..." his voice trailing off.

"No matter," Billy responded, "He's gone now, that's all that matters. I'll be seeing you sir."

With that, he put his arm around Jane and started to lead her home. She was trembling.

"You're safe now." He said.

Once they got home and settled, Billy got word to Mary and Harry that Jane was at home, then knelt on the floor by the side of Jane and said "My love, I meant every word I said back there. You are the most important person in my life. Your mum looks like she has the chance of some happiness with Harry and my parents will be just around the corner. We can get to know Alice and Ron better and make the most of our extended family. It's time for us to relax and move on to the next chapter of our lives."

Jane watched him making his speech to her and her heart filled with joy. She pulled Billy towards her in a loving embrace and said "I've never been happier. I can't wait for the next chapter."

Also By

The Reluctant Departure
As two Victorian hearts rebel an epic family saga begins.

In a daring act of defiance, Emma and James bravely elope. Alas, their pursuit of love brings with it harsh reality, as poverty swiftly shatters their dreams.

Once bathed in luxury, Emma now irons clothes to afford their next meal. Guilt gnaws at James as he faces the hardships his bride must now endure. In the midst of the turmoil, Tommy provides a soothing presence, detecting the damsel's thinly veiled grief. As Emma's once vibrant spirit dwindles into melancholy, she mysteriously vanishes, leaving James struggling with his darkest fears.

Can James salvage the love he fears he's lost? Will Emma find solace in Tommy's arms? Or is she plotting to run away a second time and start a new happier life on her own terms?

The Chaperone's Choice
A young lady and her chaperone. Two young gentlemen and an unlikely Victorian romance.

Bereaved and adrift after her father's death, reluctant Eleanor, must take a position as a lady's companion to the vivacious Lily Woodward. Thrust into a world of lavish opulence, Eleanor is neither servant nor family but a chaperone in a complex social dance.

Caught in a whirlwind of feelings, Floyd flirts with her, but it's Lily who wants him. Eleanor is drawn to Hugh, Floyd's best friend whose charm lights a spark in her heart, but he doesn't seem to even notice her.

Despite her disinterest in Floyd, his words still pierce like a dagger when she overhears him confiding in Hugh that she's nothing more than a mere diversion. When Hugh doesn't defend her honour, Eleanor's spirits crumble, leaving her to bury her blossoming feelings deep within, aching to break free.

When Hugh declares his feelings for Eleanor she assumes the worst but when Hugh's departure imminent, Eleanor stands at a crossroads. Will she unearth the truth of Hugh's affections and embrace her feelings, or allow hearsay to guide her heart, potentially missing her shot at happiness?

Delve into an enthralling saga of romantic complexities and societal norms. In the heart of Victorian England, experience Eleanor's journey as it embodies the resilience of a woman navigating love, duty, and personal growth. Unearth her story today—an ideal read for enthusiasts of women's historical fiction and family sagas.

The Motherless Child
In the Shadows of Deceit: Anna's Fight for Truth and Love.

Following a death in her family, Anna is saddled with an immense debt, forcing her into the precarious care of her conniving uncle and his family. Once dreaming of inheriting the family business, her hopes turn to ashes along with the destroyed factory, plunging her life into chaos.

Cut off from her best friend and abandoned by her fiancé, Anna endures her isolation with fortitude. Salvation appears in the form of a marriage proposal from her cousin, but beneath the surface, deceitful currents swirl.

As she's ensnared in a web of betrayal, Anna must summon her strength to reclaim her life and her love. But has the heartache pushed her past the point of no return?

Immerse yourself in Anna's captivating and emotional journey of steadfast resilience and romance. Perfect for devotees of sweeping historical fiction and riveting family sagas, this tale will delight those who relish narratives about strong women battling the odds in the British Victorian era.

The Christmas Resolution

A Tale of Love and Resilience in Victorian London

In the heart of the bustling and unforgiving streets of Victorian London, Rosie's life takes a devastating turn when a tragic factory explosion claims the lives of her parents. Left as the sole provider for her younger sister, Rosie's determination to shield her sibling from the harsh realities of life becomes her driving force.

With rent looming and resources dwindling, Rosie embarks on a perilous journey to London in search of a better future. Yet, as they navigate the grim metropolis, doubt creeps in, and Rosie questions if their dreams are nothing more than fragile illusions.

As her sister's health deteriorates, Rosie's desperation pushes her to the brink of despair, and the threat of arrest looms. Just when all seems lost, a compassionate stranger extends a helping hand, offering a glimmer of hope. But not everyone wishes them well, and Rosie finds herself back on the unforgiving streets, teetering on the precipice of survival.

In this poignant Victorian romance, Rosie's resilience is put to the ultimate test as she grapples with destitution, danger, and the unyielding pursuit of a brighter future. Will she be forever trapped in the clutches of poverty, or can the truth finally set her free, leading her to a love she never dared to dream of?

The Workhouse Child
Escaping Shadows: A Victorian Tale of Courage, Kindness, and Second Chances in Bristol

In the gritty heart of Victorian Bristol, young Annie's life unfolds within the cold, oppressive walls of the workhouse, a place she despises more than anything. When her steadfast friend and protector vanishes without a trace, leaving her alone and vulnerable, Annie believes she has no choice but to escape the confines of her grim existence. She longs for freedom, a loving family, and a chance to lead a better life outside the confines of the institution.

Her flight from the workhouse nearly ends in tragedy beneath the merciless wheels of a tram, and Annie starts to wonder if fate has forsaken her. Yet, a chance encounter with a stranger reveals a glimmer of hope, showing her that not all souls are tainted by cruelty.

But when another friend meets a tragic end, Annie is haunted by the spectre of doom. It's only the unexpected kindness of a compassionate stranger that opens her eyes to the possibility of a family she's longed for but never dared to dream of.

As justice finally begins to close in on the malevolent forces that haunt her nightmares, Annie's life seems to be turning a corner.

Yet, the twists of fate are unpredictable, and her newfound happiness teeters on the edge of uncertainty. Will she finally find the family and love she craves, or will the shadows of her past threaten to consume her once more?

In this gripping Victorian romance, Annie's journey is a testament to the enduring power of hope and the resilience of the human spirit. Perfect for those who love historical fiction and riveting family sagas.

Charlottes Predicament
A Victorian family saga: Heartbreak, second chances, and family bonds

Amidst the opulence of Victorian society, Charlotte's life takes a turbulent turn. Nanny to two beloved children, when their mother dies she's asked to assume a more significant role in their lives.

Slowly, a deep connection blossoms between Percival and Charlotte, and their love story unfolds in stolen moments and promises of a future together. When tragedy strikes and tears them apart, Charlotte faces isolation and heartbreak, with only the meagre solace of her cottage and savings.

The discovery of her pregnancy complicates matters and Charlotte is reminded of the family fortune's implications and she feels she has not choice but to let her son be brought up in the bosom of his sibling's family home.

As time goes by, she observes her son Owen growing from a distance. She is tied by a promise to the children she still cares for. Even Percival's son, Benjamin, begins to understand the love she had for his father. It's only when she meets Jonathan, another widow, that the prospect of a new life emerges.

Revealing her newfound love to the family, especially Benjamin proves challenging. Amidst family secrets and regrets, will Charlotte find the happiness and redemption she seeks in a society bound by expectations and class divisions?

In this compelling Victorian romance, Charlotte's journey is a testament to the enduring power of love, resilience, and the possibility of redemption, reminding us all that second chances are worth pursuing, no matter how unexpected they may be.

Violet's Downward Spriral
Victorian Bristol: A Tale of Theatrical Deceit and Unlikely Love

In the glittering world of Victorian theatre, a young actress named Violet shines like a star, capturing the hearts of the audience. Behind the scenes, she's entangled in a web of deception woven by Duncan, the theatre owner's son, who sees her as a pawn in his game of jealousy and ambition.

Duncan's manipulative plan unfolds, pushing Violet to the brink of heartbreak. When she's persuaded to disappear, her absence becomes a sensation. Duncan revels in the attention, believing he's proving himself to his father.

As sightings of Violet create a media frenzy, she finds herself in Dublin, seeking refuge and a chance at a new life. Her parents hope to bring her back quietly, but the media has other ideas, casting her into a spotlight she never wanted.

Amidst the chaos, a new actor, Bernard, enters Violet's life, offering the possibility of true love. But Violet's heart remains tethered to Duncan, even as he reveals his heartless intentions. When he cruelly abandons her, she spirals into despair, contemplating a tragic end by the river's edge.

Saved by a passerby, Violet's life takes an unexpected turn. Misunderstood and embarrassed, she grapples with the aftermath of her ordeal. Her parents, deeply concerned, consider drastic measures while Bernard's aunt, Lillian, steps in to offer a lifeline.

As Violet embarks on a journey to heal, Bernard's unspoken love lingers between them. Torn between her past and the potential for a future with Bernard, Violet contemplates leaving and making a new life for herself in Ireland. But as their feelings converge, a moment of courage may finally bridge the gap between them, leading to a love neither dared to dream of in the heart of the Victorian theatre world.

In this compelling Victorian romance, Violet's journey is a proof that love and resilience can make anything possible, whatever the challenges. Never giving up hope can give you more than you ever dreamed of and a future worth pursuing.

The Christmas Hope

Rediscovering Hope: A Victorian Christmas Tale of Family and Love

In the heart of Victorian London, a chance encounter at a soup kitchen on Christmas Eve alters the course of twelve-year-old Hope's life. Lost, frightened, and clutching a spoon as her only possession, she finds an unexpected saviour in a kind stranger.

Hope is taken under the wing of the benevolent gentleman, who offers her a place in his home. Yet, his wife's reluctance threatens to cast her out. As fate intervenes, Hope becomes a part of their family and flourishes.

Growing into a young woman, Hope's quiet life takes a turn when she falls in love with Samuel. However, her uncertain lineage haunts her, prompting a quest to uncover her true origins.

With the help of Samuel, Hope retraces her past, unearthing clues that lead to a soup kitchen from her childhood. As she delves deeper into the mystery, a revelation emerges—one that promises to change her life forever.

But just as Hope's future begins to crystallise, a dark figure from her past reemerges, claiming to be her father. The encounter sends shockwaves through her world, leading to a thrilling quest for the truth and a battle against sinister forces.

In this heartwarming Christmas tale, Hope's journey is one of resilience, love, and the enduring power of family, reminding us that the spirit of the season can bring miracles and second chances.

The Young Companion
Whispers of the Heart: A Victorian Romance

In the heart of Victorian Bristol, Eugenie's world shatters when her father vanishes. With the weight of responsibility on her shoulders, she secures a position as a companion to two young sisters, using her family name as her ticket.

Amidst the grandeur of her employers' home, Eugenie's love for books draws her to a secluded library, where she encounters Cedric, a fellow bookworm. Their connection blooms into a deep friendship, and the pages of their lives become intertwined.

But as the girls' brother, George, sets his sights on Eugenie, promising her the world, she's faced with an agonising choice. Reluctantly, she agrees to marry him, even as her heart yearns for Cedric. Duty to her family guides her steps.

When Eugenie's father returns unexpectedly, her carefully laid plans unravel. Faced with a momentous decision, she must choose between keeping her promise and following her heart. But as she discovers George's true nature, she's forced to confront the darkness that looms over her.

With the threat of danger looming, Eugenie's only hope lies in her brother's protection. The path she's chosen appears treacherous, yet with Cedric by her side, there's a glimmer of hope that love will ultimately light her way.

Eugenie's journey showcases the strength of love and bravery despite the presence of danger and uncertainty. Immerse yourself in this emotional journey of steadfast resilience and romance. Perfect for those who love historical fiction and riveting family sagas, this story is for those who relish narratives about strong women battling the odds in the British Victorian era.

Printed in Great Britain
by Amazon